"I KNOW IT SOUND: asking another man to kind of stupid asking."

"I offered my help and I will." Trace studied her without speaking for a moment. "I don't know exactly how to go about doing this. It's not like I know a whole lot of eligible bachelors in this town. So what would you be looking for in a husband?"

A hot rush of heat flamed up her cheeks. How could she have misunderstood his intentions? How could she have thought that maybe he wanted to marry her?

"Give me a quick rundown, we can fine-tune it later," Trace added.

"I don't really know what I'm looking for in a husband," she murmured.

"You have to know something of what you desire in a man," he encouraged her.

"He has to be kind and understanding. And because we're only doing this to protect my son, my 'husband' will have to accept that we will not consummate the relationship."

"No sex?" Trace asked. "That puts a hitch in my search."

"This is only until the courts give me full custody of Lucas. Then we'll get divorced right away," Jade said quickly.

"Oh, Jade," he asked, "what are you really looking for? A man to love? A man to love you back? I promise you, it's possible. . . ."

WHAT ARE *LOVESWEPT* ROMANCES?

They are stories of true romance and touching emotion. We believe those two very important ingredients are constants in our highly sensual and very believable stories in the LOVE-SWEPT line. Our goal is to give you, the reader, stories of consistently high quality that may sometimes make you laugh, sometimes make you cry, but are always fresh and creative and contain many delightful surprises within their pages.

Most romance fans read an enormous number of books. Those they truly love, they keep. Others may be traded with friends and soon forgotten. We hope that each LOVESWEPT romance will be a treasure—a "keeper." We will always try to publish

LOVE STORIES YOU'LL NEVER FORGET BY AUTHORS YOU'LL ALWAYS REMEMBER

The Editors

JADE'S GAMBLE

PATRICIA OLNEY

BANTAM BOOKS
NEW YORK · TORONTO · LONDON · SYDNEY · AUCKLAND

JADE'S GAMBLE

A Bantam Book / May 1998

ISBN 0-553-44609-6

Published simultaneously in the United States and Canada

Bantam Books are published by Bantam Books, a division of Bantam Dou-
bleday Dell Publishing Group, Inc. Its trademark, consisting of the words
"Bantam Books" and the portrayal of a rooster, is Registered in U.S. Patent
and Trademark Office and in other countries. Marca Registrada. Bantam
Books, 1540 Broadway, New York, New York 10036.

PRINTED IN THE UNITED STATES OF AMERICA

OPM   10 9 8 7 6 5 4 3 2 1

To R.J. and Chris,
two heroes in the making.
I love you guys.

And to R.D.O.
forever and always

ONE

"You need a husband."

Jade O'Donnell gaped at her attorney, Morris Peterson. She couldn't believe what he was telling her.

Having been married for a mere half hour before her first husband had walked out on her eight years earlier was enough to tell her that marriage didn't work for her. Why should that have changed?

"And fast," Morris added, rustling through the mountain of papers on his desk. "We have a court date that's coming up quicker than I'd like to see."

She could feel the rush of heat covering her cheeks. "Could you run that by me again, Morris? The husband part."

Morris leaned his elbows on his desk, ignoring the stack of files that fell over the edge and onto her feet. He looked straight at her.

"What I'm telling you, Jade, is that you're in one

hell of a predicament. If you got yourself a husband, I believe it would be easier to win this custody battle for your son."

"This is stupid." She picked up the files and placed them on top of the mess on his desk.

It was insane.

She didn't need any turmoil in her life. She and Lucas were nicely settled in the small and quiet tourist community of Faith, California, a few miles southwest of Lake Tahoe; and she and her aunt Ruth were working to expand their bakery, the Cinnamon Girl.

Although Morris Peterson was the only attorney in town, she still had to question herself for hiring him. Granted, she could have gone to South Lake Tahoe or Truckee to obtain the services of another attorney, but money was tight and Morris was really all she could afford. . . . Still, there were those rumors about his drinking.

"My ex-husband has been gone for eight years," she said.

"But," Morris said, holding up his hand while he talked, "we suspect that Rick is after Lucas's inheritance. We know he won't be after you per se, because your parents didn't leave you a dime. Is that correct?"

"That's right," she said, forcing back the unpleasant memories that always plagued her when she thought of her parents.

"No real property, no savings accounts, mutual funds, et cetera."

"Nothing. After my parents died in that car accident in the spring, their entire estate was left in trust to Lucas."

The lawyer clasped his hands together. "It doesn't help that you filed for bankruptcy two years ago. That guarantees you won't be appointed as successor trustee in Thorton Stevens's place once he leaves for Europe. And since the first alternate, ah . . ." He paused as though trying to gather his thoughts. "Ah, yes, I remember now. Since Allen Pearson has . . ."

"Has died," Jade finished for him.

"Yes, then the courts will have to decide who'll handle Lucas's trust fund."

"Thorton Stevens," Jade said, "was my parents' trusted friend and attorney." And he had a son, Beau Stevens, whom everyone in the two families had expected Jade to marry. Everyone except Jade.

"It concerns me," Morris said, "that with your financial history, it might appear that you're an unfit mother—"

Jade clenched her fingers into a fist. "I am a fit mother," she said, resisting the urge to slam her fist on the desk. "We've had some financial setbacks, but we're on the right track now. My business is growing, though a little slower than we'd like. But we're making progress."

Morris raised his hand again. "I know that you're a fit mother. But it might appear to a judge as though you're unable to support Lucas properly. I believe getting a husband, with the added money he'd bring in, and his being a male role model, would provide the best protection. You can contest the decisions of both the mediator and the judge if the custody fight isn't resolved in your favor, but that could run into thousands of dollars."

"Which I don't have."

"And as much as I'd like to help you, I can't. I've already adjusted my fee as low as I can."

"I want you to know I appreciate your efforts, but you have to understand my frustration. I haven't seen or heard from Rick since—"

"Since you recently started getting all these letters after your parents died," Morris said, pulling her file out of a stack she hadn't even noticed.

"Here's another one," she said. She slid the envelope across his desk.

"This makes number five to date, doesn't it?"

"Yes."

"All nonthreatening letters, correct?" he asked as he perused the note.

"Yes."

He laid the letter down. "I don't know how to make this any clearer to you. I know this sounds like a raw deal, especially when we don't know Rick's true motivation. But life isn't fair, and we have to fight any way we can. I could get an extension for the meeting with the mediator, but depending on who that mediator is, we need to be prepared. Do you understand what I'm saying?"

"Yes. I need to get a husband. And fast."

Morris nodded.

"I did everything I could over the past eight years to find Rick and terminate his parental rights," she said. "When I did locate him, he wouldn't take my calls. He never answered any of my letters."

A slow burn of anger curled up Jade's spine. Maybe she hadn't tried hard enough. Maybe there was more she could have done in the beginning.

"That's good," Morris said, gathering up some files and placing them on the oak credenza behind him. "That will help show abandonment on his part."

"So why all this?"

"The court wants to see a stable home life. A mother and a father to raise this child."

Dread gripped her. Morris was right. As far as she knew, Rick wasn't rich, but he was greedy, and San Francisco wasn't far away enough to keep him from suddenly showing up, demanding his parental rights.

Rick had known she was pregnant when Reverend Fowler had pronounced them husband and wife. Half an hour later she'd found herself at the reception, hearing him say he didn't think it was such a good idea for them to marry. They were already married, she'd thought, stunned. Wasn't it a little late?

It had been interesting, she mused, remembering her parents, Fuller and Iris O'Donnell, standing there among their handpicked four-hundred-plus Beverly Hills and Hollywood elite friends, with their perfect little girl dressed in white, pretending to be a virgin, standing by their side and being embarrassed as all hell.

What a pushover she'd been her entire life. She'd been a wimp where her parents were concerned and a wimp with Rick. But she wasn't going to let him walk all over her this time.

"Do you understand, Jade?"

Forcing down the lingering insecurities and the fears from her childhood that were still real to her, she told herself she would stand her ground no matter how weak she felt.

Her life belonged to her son.

She rose from her chair. "I understand."

"I'm sorry if this sounds a bit farfetched to you, but it's one more positive step we can take. And we only have a few weeks before the court date."

"Fine," she said, wondering who in the world she could get to marry her on such short notice.

"Perhaps you could make some sort of business arrangement with one of the men here in town," Morris suggested. "I could assist you there if you'd like."

She shook her head, trying not to laugh at the pure insanity of it all. "I think I can manage that part on my own, thanks."

"Very well. If you need me, I'm here to help."

She wiped her hand across her nose, fighting the urge to cry. She had to admit, Morris was right. This would have to be a business arrangement of some sort. It wasn't like she was supposed to fall in love and marry for good. This was for Lucas.

"I appreciate your coming in so early," she said. "I still have to make my morning deliveries, so I'm thankful for you opening before office hours."

"No problem. Anytime." He walked her to the door. "I wish you luck in your search."

A few moments later she found herself standing on the brick steps in front of the Victorian-era building facing Main Street where Morris had his office.

A trickle of sweat ran down her back. She knew it wasn't from the heat, though it was unseasonably warm for an early summer morning. If she didn't find an eligible bachelor, and soon, she could risk losing Lucas.

She didn't know what to do. What she did know was that she was in trouble.

Big trouble.

He was dreaming again.

Of a woman, naked, with long hair as black as midnight and a voice as heavenly as an angel's.

She reached for him, running alongside him, pulling him deeper into the open meadow filled with fragrant grass and surrounded by pungent pine trees, her hair flowing behind her. He couldn't see her face, but she stopped and whispered to him, her lips brushing against his ear. The spicy-sweet scent of her drew him to her, into her warm, gentle embrace. She slowly undressed him, leaving him naked, and he reached for her, wanting. He knew her skin would feel like silk and taste as luscious as golden honey.

Falling to the soft earth, he pulled her to him, but she suddenly slipped through his fingers like a fine mist, pitching him into his usual nightmare, into the inky thickness where he couldn't breathe or move.

His lungs burned, and the black smoke that was all too familiar stung his eyes. He heard their cries, but he couldn't help them. He felt the burning pain eating away at his flesh, but he couldn't move.

Instead, he let the swirling flames and acrid smoke eat him alive.

A cold spray of water woke him.

Trace Banyon shot out of bed, narrowly missing being blasted by a second shower of water through the open window. He swore as he stumbled across the finely polished wooden floor littered with the clothes he'd dropped the night before. Shaking himself from the fiery grip of his nightmare, he fumbled for a pair of sweatpants and pulled them on with one strong yank.

Another spray of water sailed through the window, past the parted flowery curtains, splashing his bare feet.

"What the hell?" He jerked open the French doors that led to the balcony off his first-floor room.

"Hey, you," he yelled, and pointed at a tow-headed boy who stood a few feet from the open window, holding a garden hose.

Startled, the boy dropped the hose, causing it to squirm and wiggle like a giant green worm in the thick grass. The hose whipped up, shooting more water across the redwood balcony and Trace's bare chest and face.

"Turn that damned thing off." He wiped the water from his face with a swipe of his hands. "Now!"

The kid stumbled and caught the edge of the wriggling hose, spraying water high into the air and onto himself. Soaked from top to bottom, he stood there for a few seconds, his huge eyes expressing his shock and surprise.

Trace leaped over the banister of the balcony and landed with a soft thud in the grass a few feet from the boy. He grabbed the rubber tube and twisted the nozzle off. Then he marched to the faucet and turned the tap.

"What do you think you're doing?" he demanded. His ears were ringing and his mouth tasted dry. He had definitely had one too many beers the night before.

The boy's lips were drawn in tight, and he clenched his fists at his sides. He didn't say a word. Instead, he chose to stare at Trace with startling green eyes that bored right through him.

"I asked you a question," he said, noting that the kid, though clearly afraid, wasn't backing down. "What were you doing squirting water through my window?" He gestured toward his room. "See that window, that wide-open window?"

"I was putting out the fire."

"What?" Quickly, he looked around for any sign

of smoke or flames as a paralyzing fear shot through him. "What fire?"

The boy pointed to Trace's room. "The one in the window."

The curtains fluttered out with the morning breeze, reminding Trace of a butterfly taking flight.

"Of all the stupid things to do," he said, his voice harsh with frustrated anger. He caught the kid's stare and noticed his shoulders were shaking. Guilt flashed through him. In a gentler tone he added, "There's no fire."

The boy gestured with both of his hands. "But the shed blew up and—and then the house caught fire."

A persistent beat pounded in Trace's left temple. "I've already told you, kid, there is no fire. If there were, you stay out of the way and let the firemen do their job." He turned to leave. "Now go away."

"But there are no firemen here to help," the boy said. "I had to do it."

Trace stopped mid-stride, feeling his heart stick in his throat. As hard as he tried, he couldn't erase the cries for help from his mind. The pain struck hard and fast. It was impossible to forget that he had failed.

Would his father, Trace wondered, a decorated and honored fire captain for the city of Bellevue, Washington, approve of the way Trace had quit the force? Would he understand how the scent of smoke brought an instant sweat of alarm? Would he feel compassion and realize that the haunting nightmares were real, that the scars left behind were on his soul as well as his body? Would he forgive his son for leaving so suddenly and not saying a word?

Trace clenched his jaw. "Let it alone."

"But someone has to."

"Look, kid, I don't care about any fires. I just want you to get out of here. Get it?"

He wished he could have said it a little less harshly, but the boy was bringing up memories he'd rather forget. He was tired and had no patience to console some little kid, who, he realized, was just being a kid.

"Sorry," the boy said in a squeaky voice, then ran around the corner of the inn, hanging on to his soggy shorts as he fled.

Trace sighed wearily as every bit of emotion drained from his body. He ached all over and his head pounded, reminding him of the party at Ike's Bar and Grill the night before. Or was it Spike's Bar and Grill? All he could remember was the deer head with its huge antlers hanging on the wall and a girl named Samantha hanging all over him. Or was it Tamara? Whatever her name was, he shouldn't have had all those beers.

Damn kid. Maybe he should find the boy and explain, but he decided against it. The damage had already been done.

Running his fingers through his dripping hair, he trudged across the lawn toward his room, intent on grabbing some aspirin, a warm shower, and dry clothes.

In that order.

"Wait just one minute!" a woman suddenly demanded from behind him.

Now what? Slowly turning around, he saw a woman who he guessed couldn't be older than thirty or taller than five-foot-three.

Boldly, she faced him, her hands planted on her trim hips. She wore a denim-and-lace jumpsuit with lace trim on her shoulders and a wide leather belt that showed off her firm stomach and small waist. The denim hugged her legs, hinting at shapely limbs underneath.

"What?" he asked, feeling trouble sparking like a lit match dropped into a dry field.

As a firefighter, he'd learned how to handle people and their problems. It was part of the job, part of his nature to help people. Not only pulling them from burning buildings and saving their homes and their memories, but he was also a medic, a counselor, and a psychologist to everyone. Everyone except himself.

Ex-fireman, he reminded himself. His career, by choice, was in the past.

The woman didn't back down from his steely stare, but instead advanced toward him.

"I want to know what all this shouting is about," she said. "And what gives you the right to yell at my son like some maniac?"

He'd also learned, in the many years of fire fighting, how to detect hot spots. And this one was hot, indeed.

She yanked her sunglasses off, causing her deep brown hair to fall out of its loose ponytail. Long, velvety tresses fell over one shoulder. Through blurry eyes, he took a moment to study her.

The early-morning summer sun illuminated her gentle profile. Translucent wide green eyes, slightly tilted at the corners, reminded him of a jungle cat. Her face was fine-boned and delicate, like the rest of her. But something told him this was one tough lady.

Determined to put her in her place, he looked back at her eyes. Then he knew. "That kid belongs to you, doesn't he?"

"Yes, I just said that, and *that kid*—my son—has a name. It's Lucas." Her voice was as intense as a fierce wind flaming an out-of-control blaze. She came at him again until they were nearly face-to-face. A frown creased her brow and a determined look darkened her eyes. "You terrified him with all your yelling and shouting. How dare you!"

"He blasted me with that damn hose, waking me out of a dead sleep. How do you think I should react?"

"With a little control."

He clamped his mouth shut, biting back a retort. He didn't want to get into a shouting match with this woman. It wasn't like him to chew out a lady, or a kid for that matter, but he'd had enough stress and guilt over the last year, enough to push anyone's temper to the limit. Besides, she had to know that he didn't appreciate her son's behavior.

"You oughta control your kid, lady."

"You oughta control your temper," she shot back. "He's only seven, and he was playing fireman. It's his dream to become a fireman someday and you yelled—"

"Tell him to forget it," Trace muttered, and turned around to head back to his room.

Dizziness and nausea hit vigorously as he moved. When would he learn that drinking wouldn't make his problems disappear? He still had the burn scars up his back and arms, still had the nightmares. The drinking hadn't brought the dead woman and her son back to life. It hadn't brought Valerie back either.

Not that he wanted Valerie back. His life was better the way it was. And that meant being alone and not falling into that age-old trap called love.

Besides, Valerie had told him she didn't want to commit her life to a man who might never come back from a call, let alone a man who was physically and emotionally scarred.

At least she'd the decency to return the engagement ring. Somehow, it had softened her words of rejection as he lay in the Seattle Burn Center recovering from his injuries.

"There are better things to do with his life," he added. To his surprise, the woman was right behind him like a wildcat on a hunt.

"What's that supposed to mean?" she asked, grabbing his arm and stopping him.

Her hand was soft, her grip firm.

Her action surprised him, and he automatically

drew back. He tried to tell himself that he didn't miss the gentle caress of a woman's hand or the emotional closeness that came with it.

He became even more belligerent. "Being a fireman isn't glamorous, it isn't a dream," he said, remembering how the yellow flames would mix with the intense black smoke, lending a dingy cast to the sky. Or how the sweep of water from overhead helicopters and the fire hoses would temporarily cool the burning inferno. Or how the searing pain of the flames ate away at his flesh while the cries for help went unanswered.

"And it isn't being a hero," he said, emphasizing the last word. "Simply put, lady, it's not worth it."

"You sound like you know what you're talking about."

Her tone was calm, as though she'd forgotten their argument. Their gazes met and held for a moment. A look of understanding flickered across her face as she stared up at him with those ever-so-green eyes of hers, eyes that were fringed with long black lashes.

"You don't know me," he said, his voice rougher than he would have wanted. "So don't try to read me."

"What's the matter with you?"

"What's the matter with—" He stopped in amazement. He'd just had the rudest awakening in his life, and this woman, this pint-sized dynamo, had the nerve to dress him down as though he were the one who'd caused the trouble.

His shoulders rose and fell with the deep breath he took. "You're crazy, you know that? No matter what excuse you make, that still was one hell of a way to wake up—"

"You still had no justification to yell at a young boy like that," she said, coming back at him with the same ferocity he'd seen earlier.

"I'd yell at anyone for doing the same. It's no excuse just because he's a kid. All the more reason for him to learn some manners."

Her green eyes flashed like lightning. "I don't mind telling you that you're one cold person," she said, her gaze sweeping over him. She took a step away as though he had some kind of disease.

He knew she had to have seen the scars covering his back when he started to leave a minute before. But did she see the scars on his soul as well?

Feeling reckless, he leaned closer to her. He wasn't sure why except something about her drew him. "Yeah, well, no kidding. I got washed down with a blast of ice water."

"I'm surprised Sue let someone like you stay at Banyon's Retreat," she said. "She's usually a better judge of character and much more discriminating as to whom she lets stay here."

One corner of his mouth lifted in a slight smile. "Is that a fact?"

A dusky rose color blossomed across her cheeks. "Lucas made a mistake," she said in a gentler tone. "I'm sure he's sorry. Did he apologize? If he didn't, then I'll apologize for him."

"Don't bother."

"You're even rude when someone tries to apologize to you. Unbelievable."

He merely stared at her, surprised by the trace of softness he saw mixed with the ferocious determination in her face.

The anger he'd seen in her eyes and heard in her voice was an emotion he could deal with. He felt a whole lot safer that way. Unlike when he saw the warmth of her expression and heard the tenderness in her voice when she spoke of her son.

Damn. He didn't like sensing vulnerability in himself. It put him at a disadvantage.

No, he couldn't handle being responsible for someone. Not now . . . not ever again.

In fact, he just wanted to be left alone.

He gave her one last look. The softness was gone. Her hair hung in disarray across her shoulders, and her stance indicated she was ready for a fight again. She was like a tigress protecting her cub.

Well, she was one wildcat he'd be sure to stay away from. No sense in being scratched.

"If you'll excuse me," he said, stepping past her. His voice was tight and strained. "I need to get a towel and dry off."

She should have been able to cut him off at the knees, Jade told herself.

Then she would have made a grand exit, satisfied

that she'd put him in his place with her wit and biting words.

Neither of which she'd done. He'd beat her to it, she thought a couple of hours later as she pulled the delivery van into the drive at the back of the bakery, only to see an unfamiliar beige pickup blocking her way.

"Man, what a morning." She let out a slow breath and rested her forehead on the steering wheel as she tried to unwind.

Her annoyance didn't stem from the incident at Sue's, but rather from the problems Rick was causing and her own lack of confidence in herself. She couldn't even stand up to a stranger. She was just like she'd always been.

Weak.

She'd been weak in dealing with her parents when they had dictated every aspect of her life, all in the name of making her presentable to their peers.

If only they could see her now with her wild mane of hair, the cutoff jeans she was fond of wearing, and her sloppy housekeeping habits. Her occasional messiness alone would merit the cold, silent treatment for a week.

She'd been equally as weak with Rick, never saying a word about his bad habits, or that blonde bimbo he'd met in La Jolla.

And when she'd discovered she was pregnant with his child, she'd believed the only solution was marriage. That way she wouldn't disgrace her family. At least that's what she had thought. So when her marriage failed, her parents had let her know their extreme disappointment in the way she'd handled herself.

To avoid further disgrace, after Rick had left her, her parents had arranged for her to live with her aunt Ruth in northern California until the baby was born and put up for adoption. Then she would be allowed to return home. Fuller and Iris O'Donnell had a reputation to uphold.

Jade opened her eyes, her annoyance increasing when she found that her hands were shaking.

She had done what her parents wished. The only differences were she had kept her son and never returned home.

Jade got out of the van and pocketed the keys. She'd dropped Lucas off at one of his friend's after leaving Sue's B and B. Her frustrated mood hadn't changed one bit as she'd made the deliveries to all their customers. And now seeing the truck blocking the entrance to the driveway wasn't helping.

Frowning, she marched into the bakery. Most everyone in Faith parked in front on the street or hitched their bicycles to the old-fashioned hitching post when they came in to get some of Aunt Ruth's cinnamon buns.

The heavenly scent of cinnamon and spice, of freshly baked vanilla swirls and sugar cookies, enveloped her the second she opened the door. She heard Aunt Ruth's loud laughter billowing down the hallway and a male voice that sounded vaguely familiar.

Turning a corner, she ran into her aunt.

"Our problems are solved," Ruth said, taking a quick breath. Her eyes gleamed with excitement, and her face was flushed a deep rose hue.

"Good," Jade said, feeling her anxieties slip away at the sight of her loving aunt. "Because you won't believe the morning I've had. First, I had my meeting with Morris, and that's a story in itself. Then I had a confrontation with the nastiest person at Sue's B and B. He was yelling at Lucas for waking him with a—"

"Jade darlin', who was yelling at Lucas?" Aunt Ruth frowned, clearly confused.

"This awful man. I don't know who he was."

"Come on in the back and tell me what happened."

Jade rubbed her hand across her brow. "I don't want to bother you now about that. I'll tell you later when everything has calmed down."

"Okay, darlin'."

"Right now I have to find the owner of the pickup that's blocking the drive. I've got to get all the trays out of the back of the van."

"I'm sure he'll move the trays for you. He's absolutely wonderful," Ruth said, with enthusiasm.

"Who?"

"The owner of the pickup."

"Aunt Ruth—"

"I can't believe he's agreed to work for us. He's the man that every woman, young and old, in Faith has been whispering about for the last several days.

The man is temptation incarnate. If only I were twenty years younger and twenty pounds thinner, I'd do my doggoned best to hitch up with that hunka-hunka of pure male—"

"Aunt Ruth, slow down." Jade reached up and tucked a wild red curl out of Ruth's face. "What are you talking about?"

"Our new contractor."

Jade's mouth dropped open. "You found someone who's agreed to finish that mess Spencer Towns left behind when we fired him?"

Ruth raised a quizzical eyebrow. "Fired? That's not how I remember it. We know why Spencer left. He was afraid we couldn't pay him."

"I know. But I still can't believe it," Jade said, the thought of a new contractor almost leaving her breathless. "You mean to tell me that months and months of looking for someone to fix the 'Project from Hell' has finally ended? It's almost unbelievable."

Ruth grinned and hugged her. "I couldn't believe it either, so I hired him on the spot. And for almost half of what the others said they'd charge. Plus he agreed to accept small payments while we're getting on our feet."

"You're kidding?"

"No, I'm not. And he appears to really know what he's doing. He has references, and I called the board of contractors to check his license and to see if there were any complaints. Nothing. He's a dream come true, Jade. And did I mention that he's heavenly to look at?"

"I guess I can forgive him then for taking my parking spot. It's about time my day went a little better. I'd love to meet our new contractor. Where is he?"

"He's out back checking the framework Spencer had done." Ruth led Jade down the hall, past the large ovens, cooling racks, and baking equipment, toward the rear of the bakery.

"He said most of the work that's been done will have to be torn down and done all over again," Ruth said in one quick breath. "But that he could probably salvage most of the wood."

"What's his name?"

"Trace Banyon."

Jade stopped in the open doorway that connected the back of the bakery to the newly framed addition and stared at her aunt. "Sue's cousin?"

"Oh, did I forget to tell you?" Ruth said, turning around. "He's from Seattle."

"Last week Sue had mentioned her cousin was coming to live in Faith, though she didn't say much more about him."

"He did some contract work in Seattle after he retired as a firefighter."

Firefighter? Jade thought. It couldn't be. But then she'd instantly recognized the burn scars trailing up the stranger's well-muscled arms and back.

Before she could ask Ruth another question, a

tall, sturdy-looking man rounded the corner and nearly knocked her to the sawdust-covered floor.

He grasped her arms to prevent her from falling.

She drew in a breath as she stared into those familiar, watchful cool blue eyes.

"You!"

"You!"

TWO

The loud crack of splintering wood echoed throughout the bakery.

The muscles in Trace's shoulders burned with an ache he hadn't felt in several months. Being a firefighter had taught him the rigors of tough, dangerous work, and he'd pushed himself to his limit during the last four days since he came to work at Aunt Ruth's.

Unfortunately, even the strenuous work of hauling lumber and sacks of concrete mix under the summer sun didn't stop the obsessive nightmares that came every night.

He grunted loudly, and another crooked strip of wood flew across the floor and into the growing pile of other discarded planks. At least he'd be able to save some of the wood from the botched job that Spencer Towns had started to do.

Out of the corner of his eye, he saw a flash of

movement and frowned. Not again. "Lucas," he called. "Is that you?"

The golden-haired boy peeked around the corner. He hesitantly leaned inside the entrance of the framed addition as though waiting to be invited into a sanctuary, stopping momentarily to rub at a mosquito bite on his ankle with his other foot.

Trace sensed the boy was leery of him, and at the same time he seemed fascinated, too.

"I told you before, Lucas," he said, removing his leather work gloves and tossing them into his toolbox. "It's not safe for you to be around here with all the repair work going on." He reached for the glass of lemonade Aunt Ruth had brought earlier, and took several long swallows before placing the tumbler on a nearby stool.

"Does your mom know you're out here?"

Drawing a face in the sawdust with the toe of his sneaker, Lucas shook his head.

Trace took in a deep breath. As much as the kid reminded him of another innocent little boy, seeing Lucas and his mother interact with each other during the last four days was proof to him that life did go on.

Lucas stared at the ground. "I just wanted to know how you got so strong."

Trace paused for a second. Strong. What did the word mean, anyway? he wondered. Did winning all those firefighting awards and merits prove that he was strong? No, they didn't mean a damn thing, he decided, because being strong in spirit and strong in heart was what being a man was really all about.

"I take good care of myself," he said after a few seconds. "Ah . . . and I eat all my vegetables, that sort of thing."

He walked across the floor and crouched in front of Lucas, grasping the boy's hands. He felt strange protective emotions go through him at the touch of the boy's hands.

He briefly closed his eyes. He would welcome the stirring of anger instead, because whenever Lucas was around, he was reminded of the boy and his mother who had died.

"You know, Lucas," he said, looking into a pair of green eyes that reminded him of a certain fiery woman. "Being a good person is more important than anything. That's why I'm glad you understood why I was so upset the other morning."

"My mom and Aunt Ruth tell me not to be mad sometimes."

"That's good advice. But more important," Trace added, "it takes a strong person to admit when he's wrong."

Lucas stared at him for a moment as though judging him for all his past sins.

"And that's why I'm glad you accepted my apology," Trace finished.

Lucas dropped his gaze and shuffled from foot to foot. He gave a huge sigh.

"Okay, well, maybe you haven't." Trace stood. "I have to get back to work."

Lucas's head shot up.

The pleading look in the boy's eyes awakened yet

another emotion deep inside him, weakening him. Showing any interest wasn't a good idea, but a lot of his decisions lately had been questionable. And somehow he had to convince the boy that everything was all right between them. "Okay. Would you do me a favor and hand me my work gloves?"

Lucas didn't move, obviously not sure what to do.

"It's okay, Lucas. You can come in, but be careful where you step."

Lucas inched his way across the room to Trace's toolbox. "Did you get strong 'cause you were a fireman?"

The unexpected question caught him off guard.

Trace swung around and knocked over the stool, sending the glass of lemonade flying in one direction and the stool in another. He jumped in a fruitless effort to catch the falling tumbler. His fingers touched the glass just as it shattered against the concrete foundation. Red-hot pain seared through his hand as three large pieces of glass sliced into his palm.

Swearing to himself for being so careless, Trace managed to pull out two of the larger slivers wedged between his thumb and forefinger, but the third piece was lodged deep in his flesh. Blood oozed from the wounds.

Lucas's eyes widened. "I'll get my mom," he shouted, running toward the door.

"No, Lucas, wait a minute. I don't need any

help. . . ." Trace's voice trailed off. He knew Lucas, in his enthusiasm, hadn't heard a word he'd said.

Sighing heavily, he walked over to his toolbox, intent on finding a pair of needle-nose pliers.

"Are you hurt?"

Spinning around at the sound of Jade's soft and husky voice, he softly whistled under his breath.

She was wearing cutoff jeans and a cropped shirt that showed off her stomach, and her cheeks and chin were covered in a fine dusting of flour. Her mahogany hair cascaded over her shoulders like a veil, catching the rays from the afternoon sun. A warm glow enveloped her like a halo, knocking him emotionally off balance. If there were a heaven, he decided, then she would be an angel.

She blinked in confusion. "Oh," she said in surprise when she saw the blood dripping from his hand. "You are hurt." She came to his side.

She smelled spicy and sweet, like cinnamon.

Sweat dripped off his forehead and his heart began to pound. His hand burned with an aching heat.

This wasn't smart, he decided.

It hadn't been smart taking the job either, though he needed the money to supplement his savings. He couldn't shake the emotional draw he felt toward Jade whenever he saw her working in the bakery or playing with Lucas. And it wasn't getting any easier.

Something told him that he needed to stay as far away from Jade and her son as he could. But then just looking at her, he saw an irresistible sweetness and sincerity. She had eyes that matched her name, and a boy who was worming his way under his defenses and into his heart.

He took a calming breath and tried to convince himself that he was reacting to the sliver of glass embedded in his right hand, and not the fact that he couldn't remember ever in his life seeing anyone more beautiful than Jade O'Donnell.

Jade didn't look up into Trace's face as she examined his wound, though she could feel his gaze boring into her.

"How'd this happen?" she asked, carefully avoiding his touch. She reached for the odd-looking pliers he held.

"I slipped and dropped my glass of lemonade."

Holding the pliers in both hands, she looked at him. He towered over her and had that lean and hungry look she'd seen before. He had a presence that was known the instant he stepped into the bakery. And it was clear he was used to hard work, if his strong body and rugged look told the truth.

"Uh-huh," she said in disbelief. "Something tells me that you're not that clumsy." Far from it, she mused. He had the body and grace of a well-conditioned athlete.

As discreetly as she could, she let her gaze scan him as she tried to think of something to say that would ease her awkwardness.

His broad shoulders stretched against the faded work shirt he wore. The sleeves were rolled to his elbows, revealing muscular forearms and tanned skin. The shirt, unbuttoned at the collar, exposed some skin and a hint of muscle, giving her a glimpse of too much masculinity she'd rather not think about.

A rich mix of cut green wood, sawdust, perspiration, and the faint scent of musk aftershave came to her. His black hair touched the back of his collar. He needed a haircut as well as a shave.

"Was Lucas in here again?" she asked. She looked intently at his wound, trying to concentrate on her task rather than his blue eyes.

"Lucas?" He shrugged indifference.

"He was, wasn't he? I've told him to leave you alone."

"I don't want to run interference between mother and son, but it's okay." His voice dropped low enough to send shivers up her arms. "He can come in here as long as I'm around. I don't want him to hurt himself."

She told herself to remain calm when the only thing she felt was the room closing in on her and the strong presence of a man she was growing more and more attracted to. "Yeah, you're a good example. Like I can trust you to take care of my son."

He chuckled softly, bringing her attention back to him. The deep rumble of his laugh eased a little of her discomfort, and she grinned.

"This is nothing," he said, motioning to his wounded hand. "I promise when Lucas is here helping me nothing will happen to him."

His words were comforting, and she believed he meant what he said. She wanted to thank him, but she couldn't say a word. Instead, she glanced down at his hand.

"I have a first-aid kit in the back of my truck," he said.

"And we have one inside the bakery."

Concentrating on the last piece of glass in his hand, she kept telling herself not to look at him.

"I can handle this," he said.

"Oh, you can, can you?" Without thinking, she looked directly into his eyes. It was a mistake.

The corners of his mouth curled slightly, causing her to take in a deep breath.

Aunt Ruth had kept the rumor mill going with every one of her customers, chatting about the rugged, handsome stranger she'd hired, swearing that he was as tempting as sin. Jade would roll her eyes at her aunt's exaggeration, but standing this close to him, she finally admitted to herself just how tempting he was.

It was crazy, she thought, how in the last several days she'd tried to avoid him but couldn't. How could she, with her working in the bakery every day and Trace right down the hallway?

Every time she'd turn around, he was there, watching her with his intense blue eyes. When she needed a helping hand, he was there. He never complained and never had a discouraging word to say. Only a smile or two and then he'd go back to work, sawing and hammering away at the "Project from Hell."

She had to admit he was downright good-looking. Those sharp blue eyes of his, she bet, didn't miss a thing, and she was sure his wide sensual mouth could tempt the deepest secrets out of any female. That was enough to tell her he was one dangerous man. And now, to be close enough to feel the heat from his body, to inhale his unique aroma, she realized just how much danger she could get into.

"You really don't have to go to all this trouble," he protested. "I've been trained to handle emergencies."

"Hold still." She grasped the edge of the glass sliver with the pliers. "You're bleeding all over the floor."

"Do you always come to a person's rescue?" he asked, his voice hoarse.

"Ah, well . . . This—this is an on-the-job accident," she said, stumbling for words. "And I'm responsible for your well-being. I don't want to be in the middle of any lawsuit." With one quick tug, she pulled the splinter out.

"Ouch!"

"I'm sorry. Did that hurt?" she asked, stepping away from his compelling closeness.

"Yeah, it hurt. But I'll live."

"Good." She headed for the door. "There's antiseptic in the first-aid kit in the kitchen. Better come inside and put something on that before an infection sets in. Wrap it up good."

"I'll do that. Thanks."

"Aunt Ruth made lunch and insists that you eat."

He gave her one of his sexy smiles, showing dazzling white teeth she hadn't noticed before.

He wrapped his hand in a bandanna he fished out of his toolbox. "Tell her thanks and that I'll look forward to joining you guys in just a minute."

"I, ah, I won't be able to this afternoon. . . ." She struggled to find the words that would show she wasn't as interested in him as she really was. "I told Aunt Ruth I already had plans."

"I'm sorry to hear that."

She was keenly aware of his scrutiny. She swallowed and forced more strength into her voice. "You mind me asking why you took this job?"

The light in his eyes faded a bit. "I need the money."

Who didn't? In her office, she had her own growing pile of bills waiting to be paid.

"There's this piece of property near the lake I'd like to rent and maybe buy," he went on. "Stan Dryer owns it. I'm sure you know him."

Jade nodded. She knew exactly what property he was talking about, too. Everyone in town knew the Dryer place, a secluded cabin that oozed warmth and charm. Stan had designed and built it especially for his wife, Effie. After she died earlier that year he'd put the property up for sale.

Though not very big, the cabin sat on a knoll overlooking the south end of Lake Tahoe and was shrouded with ponderosa pine and red fir. Jade had seen the cabin and property, with its spectacular view, many times when she and Lucas had hiked along some of the trails near the lake.

Trace continued. "When Aunt Ruth asked me if I'd be interested in this messy job, I couldn't turn her down. You might say it was the pleading in her voice that convinced me."

"Did she make us sound that desperate? Because we were."

He grinned. "No, I just need the work."

She felt foolish for asking and realized that it wasn't wise to discuss anything personal with him. The less she knew about him, the better off she was. Everyone had problems, but for some reason, knowing that he did, too, only created a stronger connection between them. A bond. She didn't need anything from him except to finish the Project from Hell.

"This is your business, too, isn't it?" he asked.

"Yes, I have a small percentage. But Aunt Ruth has the final say as to what happens. I might disagree with her from time to time—"

"Which you did about her hiring me."

She clamped her mouth shut.

"Hey, look," he went on, "I know we started off kind of rough, but if it makes you feel any better, I'm not proud of how I treated Lucas or the way I talked to you the other morning. I'd had too many beers the night before. A hangover is hard to handle."

"It's okay," she said, feeling genuine warmth in him. Why was it, she mused, that a simple, sincere apology from him had her toes curling and her heart fluttering? "Forget it."

"I've told Lucas how I felt about what happened, and I did tell him I was sorry."

"I know. He told me."

Several times Jade had caught Lucas watching Trace's every move. Even Aunt Ruth had noticed and had mentioned to Jade that what Lucas needed the most was a positive male role model. A father.

Her stomach tightened as Morris's words reverberated through her mind. She wondered what Trace would be like as a father . . . and a husband.

"You had every right to rip into me that morning," he said, his gaze lingering on her mouth, then lifting back to her eyes. "And I do apologize for my rotten behavior."

She wrapped her arm around her waist in a futile effort to protect herself from the soft sound of his voice and the friendly look in his eyes.

"Your lunch is getting cold," she said, and slipped out of the room, her nerves stretched to their limit.

Trace walked down the hallway of Banyon's Retreat early the next morning, the scent of fresh-brewed coffee and cinnamon buns filling the cozy inn.

He'd been surprised at his own disappointment when Jade had run out the day before, after his accident. She hadn't eaten lunch at the bakery, and he hadn't seen her for the rest of the day.

He was continually stunned by the unexpected, fervent sensations that surged through him whenever she was near, especially after a year of struggling with his pain and guilt, until he was content to be by himself and alone in his work. He'd told himself that it didn't make sense, except something about Jade intrigued him.

Aunt Ruth, he'd soon discovered, was a talkative, tough ol' gal who'd told him over the homemade chicken soup and grilled-cheese sandwiches the day before that she, like Jade, had been cast off by the O'Donnells as the black sheep of the family.

When he asked why, she hadn't elaborated, other than to say the O'Donnells were overly concerned with convention and that she wasn't.

But that much Trace had known. One look at Aunt Ruth, with her generous, flowing red hair, her hippielike long skirts, her excessive use of Western-style jewelry, and her boisterous, loving nature, was enough to tell him that she wouldn't fit in with a rich, conservative crowd. She looked like a painter or a sculptor who should be living in a cabin in Big Sur.

But the last piece of information, concerning Jade being thrown out of the family fold, had Trace listening with renewed interest as he ate his lunch. He'd also learned that Lucas, and not Jade, was the heir of the "Morning Dawn Coffee" dynasty.

He'd read that the founder of the company, Fuller O'Donnell, and his wife, Iris, had been killed in a car accident in southern Georgia earlier that year. It was tragic, but also interesting that they hadn't left anything to their only child, Jade.

And what was equally interesting was that Jade didn't complain about the lack of money. It only seemed to spur her on, making her work harder. He admired that in her, and realized that he didn't admire Valerie for the very same thing.

At the end of the hallway, he nodded at a couple of Sue's guests. He rounded the corner to the breakfast area. Behind the swinging doors that led to Sue's bright yellow kitchen, he could hear voices.

Sue's voice and another familiar voice.

Smiling, he pushed the door open with his good hand.

Jade stood by the kitchen sink, as she did every day after making her regular morning delivery to the inn, with a coffee mug in her hand. He had hoped, as he had for the past four mornings, that he'd see her again, if only briefly before going to work at the bakery.

The rays of sunlight slanted through the kitchen blinds, casting a soft glow across her face and setting her dark hair afire.

Her deep emerald gaze locked with his, stirring his imagination. For a moment he thought he saw a hint of a passionate nature in her eyes. He could see her uneven breathing, almost feel the subtle change in the air the moment he walked in.

She tilted her head, averting her gaze from his. He watched her for a few seconds, noting the line of her chin and the softness of her full lips. Could they be as sinfully inviting as they looked? He'd bet a hundred bucks they were.

"Hey, mornin', cousin," Sue said, handing him a mug of black coffee. She brushed aside a lock of her wavy brown hair, then shoved her hand in a huge yellow oven mitt. Opening the oven door, she pulled out a tray of bubbling cinnamon rolls.

"Morning," he said, and nodded in Jade's direction, catching her glancing at him when she thought he wasn't looking.

She tugged at her bottom lip with her teeth as a dusky pink blush suffused her cheeks. She wasn't as good as she thought at disguising her emotions. Though he had to admit, her performance wasn't all that bad.

Sue, dressed in a long flowered skirt and a sleeveless white blouse, walked to the sink and turned on the water. "We've got fresh cinnamon rolls, pecan coffee cake, and homemade jams and jellies for breakfast, which should be ready in about five minutes."

"Sounds good," he said.

Sue turned to Jade, her brown eyes gleaming with curiosity. "So are you going out with him again or not?" she asked. She ran her hands under the stream of water and grabbed a towel. "He really has a thing for you, you know. A good old-fashioned crush."

"No, I didn't know," Jade said quietly. "How can he have a crush on me? We've barely started dating."

Trace took a quick swig of his coffee as he looked at Jade. He could hear the puzzlement in her voice.

"My mother always told me not to go out with boys you'd be ashamed to marry," Sue said. "So what do you say? Is he the marrying kind?"

"Sue!" Jade exclaimed. "It's just been a week."

"So?"

Jade shrugged. "I don't know. Maybe."

Trace choked on his coffee. A twinge of envy mixed with annoyance sprinted through him. "You date a man for only a week and you're already talking marriage?"

Sue laughed. "We do get married here, you know."

"Oh, yeah? But in a week?"

Sue laughed again and shook her head. "No, I'm just talking. We're not that small of a town. And we're not all desperate women who throb after anything new in town that wears pants."

He grimaced.

"You've heard the stories, too, I take it?"

"Yeah." She pulled the crock of butter out of the refrigerator. "Cindy Miller and Tamara Wilkes are the two latest females you can add to your list of admirers."

Ah, Tamara. That was her name. "Great," he muttered.

Sue looked over at Jade. "You wouldn't believe how many women, just in the short time he's been here, are after him. They say it's his cute little butt. I don't see it. He's just my cousin who, with my big brother Drake, would throw rotten apples at me when I'd follow them around."

Trace sat in one of the ladder-back chairs. "Don't listen to her, Jade. I'm a confirmed bachelor. And nothing is going to change that."

"I hear hearts breaking all over Faith." Sue threw him a glance that told him she didn't believe a word he said.

"And Sue's the one with the baseball arm," he went on, "wielding rotten apples." He turned his attention back to his cousin. "Besides, I was just wondering who would grab Jade's attention. She seems too involved in her work to notice there are men around."

Jade put her mug in the sink with a clunk. "You two don't have to talk as though I'm not here. And if it's any of your business, Trace, which it isn't, Kit Moreland has asked me for coffee a couple of times, that's all. It's not that big a deal."

He frowned at her sudden prickliness. "Kit Moreland? The owner of the hardware store?"

Jade folded her arms across her chest and her eyes narrowed. "Well . . . yes."

Something wasn't right here, he thought, feeling an odd sense of jealousy. "Isn't he a little old for you?"

She propped her hands on her hips, drawing the scoop-necked blue-and-white shirt she wore danger-ously low over her breasts. "He is not."

Trace swallowed and averted his attention to his coffee. Every time he looked into her eyes, he felt as though he was staring into a bottomless well. "So, how old is he, then? He looks fifty-something."

Surprised he'd even asked the question, he told himself that he didn't really want to know how old Kit Moreland was. What did he care if she dated, who she dated, and how old or young her dates were?

"I don't think this is any of your business, Trace Banyon," she said. She picked up the empty bakery trays and headed for the back door.

"Hey, Jade, wait," he said, jumping up, still holding his coffee mug. "Are you going right back to the bakery?"

"Yes, why?"

"I need a ride."

She looked at him as though she didn't know how to answer. "You have wheels," she said. "What's wrong with them?"

"A fan belt slipped in the truck's engine, and I haven't had a chance to get to Kit's Hardware for a new one."

Her eyebrows rose in disbelief. "So you think I'm going to rescue you again, huh?"

He thought he saw a brief smile cross her face and then disappear. Before he could answer her, she turned toward the door.

"Okay," she said. "But I'm leaving now."

She left before he could thank her, letting the screen door slam shut behind her.

Trace took the last swallow of his coffee and handed Sue his mug. He opened the door and picked up his toolbox that was sitting outside on the redwood porch. "Was it something I said?"

Sue dried her hands on a yellow towel. "She's a little sensitive about this dating stuff. She hasn't gone out much since her husband dumped her, the jerk."

"Why'd he do that?"

Sue shrugged. "It's a long story. Bottom line is, the guy's a jerk. And now Jade's fighting a custody battle for Lucas."

"Really?" He let out a slow sigh. "Aunt Ruth didn't mention anything about that."

"That's not the half of it," Sue said quickly as they heard Jade's delivery van fire up and the horn honk. "According to her lawyer, it'd be in her best interest if she provides a stable home life, in the court's view, for Lucas."

"What's that mean?"

"It means that she has to find herself a husband."

"And Kit Moreland is her answer?" Trace asked in disbelief.

So Jade had her problems, too, he mused, making her more real and human. Another one of life's little curves.

He didn't like any of this. His asking some stupid questions about a man she was dating, a man she might marry, had her eyes clouding over with despair.

"What about Lucas?" he asked. "It has to be rough on the poor kid having to go through this as well."

"I'm not sure Jade has much choice right now,"

Sue said. "She loves that boy more than you can imagine. She'll do anything for him."

"Even marry a guy she doesn't care about?"

Sue sighed. "Yeah. Even marry a guy she doesn't care about."

THREE

"Hello, again."

Pleasantly startled by the sound of his voice, Jade stopped in the doorway of Banyon's Retreat the next day. She'd been looking for Sue, but she found Trace instead, sitting in the living room in one of the over-stuffed plaid sofas that faced the stone fireplace.

Holding the door ajar with her foot, she quickly scanned the huge room, the burled-wood-carved stairway that led to the second level, and the adjacent game-and-trophy room.

They were alone.

A warm breeze stirred through the door and several open windows, bringing the tangy scent of bar-becued hamburgers and chicken and the sounds of muffled conversation and laughter from the picnic area near the lake.

"We shouldn't be having these secret encounters

like this, you know," he said, his mouth curving into a teasing grin. "Sue's guests will talk."

Jade stepped inside; her back pressed against the heavily carved door. "Really? And what do you suppose they'd say?"

"That maybe we were lovers."

She stared at him, stunned but also intrigued.

Dressed in denim jeans and a soft-looking black T-shirt, he'd showered and shaved since she'd last seen him working at the bakery earlier that day.

"Just kidding," he said.

She cleared her throat. "Ah, Sue said she'd be back from Timber Cove's by six. Is she around? We're going to a movie."

"Timber Cove's?" he asked, grabbing an apple out of a white wicker basket that sat in the center of the pine coffee table.

She watched his large hands rub the skin of the apple, the play of his strong fingers as he twisted the stem out of the fruit before pulling a small jackknife out of his back pocket. For a second she wondered about his strong and capable hands and how they'd feel rubbing and massaging away all her hurts and troubles.

"I keep forgetting you're new in town," she said, her mind snapping back to the present. "Timber Cove's Dry Cleaners."

"Ah." He cut off a slice of the apple and ate it. "Well, Sue's not here."

Against her better judgment, she watched his mouth as he continued to eat the apple. She let the magic of her imagination take hold as she dreamed about what tantalizing delights he could do with that mouth of his, even though she knew she shouldn't. She'd never had such blatantly sensual thoughts about a man before, and they tended to throw her off balance and make her a little dizzy.

And mad at herself.

As attractive as Trace was, he wasn't husband material. He wasn't the marrying kind. Despite the fact that Lucas was growing attached to him, Trace wasn't the right man.

And Lucas was a problem in himself, she realized for the hundredth time. How was she going to find a husband, any husband, and not have Lucas affected when the marriage ended?

"I'd better be going, then," she said, pushing the troubling thought aside. She opened the door. "I'll come back in a little while."

"Why don't you just wait? You're early," he said. "Fifteen minutes early. I'm sure Sue won't be long. Stay, keep me company."

Turning around, she caught him watching her. He smiled. His request puzzled her even more than the fact that, though she knew she should march right out and leave him sitting there, she didn't move an inch. If she stayed, it would be emotionally dangerous for her, although she couldn't help being attracted to him. Instead, she found herself mesmerized by the soft tone of his voice, a voice that told her maybe he'd understand and help.

She forced herself to concentrate. It was foolish.

No, she was foolish to think that a stranger would care one bit about her troubles and her growing desperation. All he'd asked was if she would stay and keep him company. If Trace were like Rick, he'd laugh in her face if he knew the depth of her problems.

"There's plenty of company down there," she said. At his frown, she nodded toward the lake. "It's beautiful down by the water at this time of day. The sun is beginning to set, and if you look just right, you can catch the rays bouncing through the pine trees."

He rose and walked across the living room, the sound of his footsteps silenced by the handwoven rugs scattered across the hardwood floor. He stopped a few feet from her.

"You sound like a romantic, Jade O'Donnell."

His whiskey-rough voice set her blood simmering.

"Are you?" He dropped the apple core in a small wastepaper basket behind her.

She flinched at the hollow sound, doing her best to ignore the heat in his question, the fire in his eyes. "I wouldn't know. I've sworn off men."

"That's too bad," he murmured, his voice wrapping around her shoulders like a soft cashmere sweater.

She opened the front door wider, telling herself she had to leave. With the little experience she'd had in her twenty-eight years, she knew enough to sense trouble, and Trace was the kind of trouble she was positive she couldn't handle.

With an easy stride, he took the last few steps that separated them and shut the door, forcing her into the inn. With a nudge of his hand against the small of her back, he guided her to a matching chair next to the plaid couch. His touch was light, but strong. And hot, burning her through the thin fabric of her cotton dress.

He eased his muscled frame onto the sofa.

"The guests are all having dinner," she said. "Why aren't you? I understand Sue's chef's barbecued chicken is pretty good."

"Too crowded for me."

"So you're a loner?" she asked, wondering about his past and what had brought him to Faith. She remembered the scars on his back and upper arms, and had noticed that, except for that first morning, he was never without a shirt, even when the sun reached its zenith. "I suppose that's a personal question. Forget it."

"No, not really," he said. "I don't mind. Right now I like the solitude. I have a lot on my mind that needs sorting out."

"Your contracting business?"

This was absurd, she thought. Why was she asking? She didn't intend to get close to any man except to find one who would agree to a quick and temporary marriage. A man like Trace Banyon could disappear out of her life as swiftly as he had shown up. If he did choose to stay in Faith, she doubted he'd ever notice her among the countless, adoring females in town.

"Yeah," he said in answer to her question, though she sensed he was lying.

"How's your hand?"

"All right." He raised the bandaged hand. "You must have a secret yen to be a nurse."

"Why would you say that?"

"You pulled that glass splinter out of my hand like a pro."

He shifted his weight, leaning his elbow on the arm of the sofa. His movements brought the light scent of soap and shampoo to linger in the summer air between them.

"You know," he said, "in the short time I've been here, I can see that you love your son and you work hard."

She felt her cheeks burn. His compliments were making her uneasy.

"You're blushing," he said. "You look good in red."

"Yeah, well." She tried to find something to say that would lighten her discomfort. "It's all part of living in a small town. You do what you can for your neighbors."

"Then you fit right in here. I've heard that you'll drop whatever you're doing to help whoever needs it. Whether it's heading a fund-raiser for improving the town square with new bricks and paint, or taking care of Mrs. Ellison's rose garden when she's laid up with a broken arm. Or even helping an injured carpenter who has a sliver of glass in his hand."

She couldn't look at him. Her gaze was riveted

on the basket of fruit in the center of the coffee table, her mind still on the color of his eyes, which were so much like the rich blue of a morning sky.

"Where did you hear all that?" she asked, telling herself she wasn't flattered by his apparent interest in her.

"Around."

"Have you been asking about me?"

"Maybe."

She jerked her gaze to his. Why would he be asking about her?

Every day, her attraction to him deepened and intensified just enough for her to notice and anticipate seeing him. And each time she did see him, the pull was stronger, even though she kept reminding herself such an attraction could be risky. He wouldn't marry her, and that was what she had to focus on. "It makes me sound like I'm a saint or something. I'm not."

"I bet you were a straight-A student and did everything your mother asked you to do."

"I didn't," she said. "At least that's what my parents would tell you if they were still alive."

"So what do you do that's so bad?"

She shrugged. "I don't always pick up after myself, and I've been known to let the dinner dishes go unwashed until the next day. All of which would have driven my parents crazy."

"Couldn't please them? Is that it?"

His curiosity touched her. It seemed so genuine. "They wanted the best for me, I'm sure," she said. "The dance lessons, charm school, that sort of stuff. There was a lot of money in my mother's family. She was a national ice-skating champion in the sixties. She was very pretty and talented. But I was all arms and legs when I was growing up, uncoordinated, clumsy, and very frustrating to them because I couldn't do anything right. I'd get embarrassed if you'd look in my direction—"

"Like now?"

"I guess I'm still shy," she admitted. "I'd nearly die if a guy asked me out. Consequently, hardly any did, except for Rick—he's my ex-husband—in college. He would shower me with compliments and do anything for me. He was the first person to really pay attention to me. I guess I was swept off my feet. My parents hated Rick from the start, and hated him more the day I married him. They had planned for me to marry the son of a family friend."

"Did you marry Rick to spite your parents and not because you loved him?"

She nodded, surprised by his perceptiveness. "Looking back, I can see that Rick wasn't really in love with me any more than I was in love with him. He was in love with my family's money. So, you see, I'm not the saint people make me out to be."

"I suppose you have a point," he said, leaning back and stretching his long legs in front of him. "But you sure as hell can shout up a storm when you're defending your son. Lord help the person who messes with him."

Pain and fear shot through her at his words.

If there was one thing her parents had been right about, it was Rick's character. The hurt and disappointment her parents had caused her didn't compare with the trouble Rick could stir up. He was going to take Lucas if she didn't do something soon.

"Jade? Are you okay? What'd I say?"

"Yeah . . . yeah, I'm fine." She brushed back her hair with shaky fingers.

"Sure?"

"It's nothing."

"Uh-huh," he said, the skepticism clear in his voice. "So, how was your date with Kit Moreland?"

Heat crawled up her neck, flushing her face all the way to her hairline. She shot him a glance she hoped told him that she really didn't want to talk about it.

"Fine," she lied.

As far as she was concerned, the date had been a disaster, enough for her to know that she could never marry Kit. Time was running out, though. She needed to find a husband quickly, and she knew Trace wouldn't do. She was simply too attracted to him. She had no intention of getting emotionally involved with a temporary husband.

He placed his hands on her bare knees and squeezed slightly. His rough fingertips grazed along her skin, sending electric sparks shooting up her legs.

She crossed her legs and leaned back, easing away from his burning touch. She didn't want to want him, emotionally or physically.

"I didn't mean to pry into your personal life," he said. "I'm just concerned about you."

"Since when? You don't know me."

"Maybe not. But I know you well enough to know that you don't have to marry a man too old for you."

He'd hit the problem head-on. She could hear her ex-husband's threats in her mind, see him taking her beloved son away from her.

She wanted to believe Trace. She wanted someone, anyone, even Trace, to take this heavy burden from her and free her and her son. For a second, as she looked at him, she wanted to crawl into his strong, capable arms for protection, and for the passion she'd never known.

"Come on, Jade," he said, his voice soft and caring. "Sue told me about your ex and Lucas. And if you think Kit Moreland is your answer, then, well, all right. But—"

"Kit was polite and considerate the entire time we had dinner at Mildred's Moonlight Café. He likes Lucas and would be a wonderful provider. And he isn't nearly as old as you think."

Though that wasn't really the problem, she suddenly thought. The intrigue, the mystery between her and Kit . . . well, there just wasn't any.

She sighed. There wasn't even a tiny spark of interest, at least on her part. Kit was too nice and polite. She didn't really want to marry him. She couldn't risk hurting him knowing that she couldn't return his feelings.

Resigning herself to the fact that she and Kit weren't an item, she looked into Trace's eyes.

Mistake, her mind screamed. Her heart pounded a wild beat.

"Isn't there another way to keep your son instead of marrying a man you don't love?" he asked.

"If I had lots of money to fight Rick in court, maybe. But I don't have the money. I can barely afford the lawyer I have. I'm convinced finding a husband is the only way to secure my son. It'd be a business contract. In fact, I probably wouldn't even tell Lucas the details in order to minimize his sense of loss and confusion when the marriage ended. Strictly business, that's all."

"If you think Kit Moreland is the one, then I say go for the man. But have you told him your real intentions?"

She didn't answer.

Trace nodded. "I suppose if you could explain your reasons for wanting to marry as quickly as possible and that it would be a marriage in name only, he'd understand. Wouldn't he?"

"You are despicable. You're—"

"Yeah, but am I right?"

She let her head drop into her hands and groaned. "Yes. You're right."

"I thought so."

Lifting her head, she caught him staring at her. He simply unnerved her with the looks he threw her way. "But I really don't want to hurt Kit. He's a nice, sensitive man who likes me more than I can possibly like him."

"I think I understand." He paused. "I can help, if you want."

Jade smiled wryly. "You're joking, of course."

He shook his head.

"I can't wait to hear this."

"What would you say if I told you I'll help you find a husband?"

At first, she was too startled by his suggestion to offer any objections. "I don't think you understand," she began just as Sue walked in the front door.

"Hi, everyone," she said, laying down the plastic-covered clothes she held in her arms. "You ready to go, Jade?"

Jade stood, but ignored Sue and pressed home her point with Trace. "This is serious, Trace Banyon. This is not a joke. I could lose Lucas."

"I'm not joking."

"Then I don't understand. What do you mean?"

He stood, barely giving her enough room to breathe. "That maybe you could marry for the right reasons," he murmured.

Jade felt the color leave her face as she suddenly realized what he was saying. Could he possibly be volunteering for the job? Was this his way of saying he wanted to marry her?

Or was she wishing for the impossible?

"Jade," Sue said. "I think we should go. The movie is gonna start in twenty minutes and you know how I like to get a center seat."

"Hey," Trace said, raising his hands, "think about it. The idea might grow on you."

Jade watched him walk to the screen door that led toward the backyard and lake. He seemed genuinely concerned, but why? "I . . . uh, I appreciate your offer."

He waved his hand and nudged the screen open. "Okay."

The last thing Jade heard was the closing of the door as he left.

With one solid swing of the hammer, Trace sank the nail home. He rubbed his index finger over the wood, knocking away some of the chips.

Placing the near-finished flower box on the concrete floor of the bakery addition, he reached for the sander. He liked the feel of creating and building something useful out of nothing. And staying late in order to finish the planter boxes for the picky Martha Jacoby was easier once he'd decided that leaving all his tools at the bakery was better than hauling them back and forth from the inn.

The sander roared to a start. Slanting the sander belt with the grain of wood in one direction and then another, he polished the job off in minutes.

Pleased with the results, he picked up the flower box to examine it closely. Smiling, he knew Martha Jacoby couldn't complain this time.

In the short time he'd been there, he'd learned that Faith was a nice town filled with good-hearted people. And since he'd started working at the Cinnamon Girl, he'd accomplished a lot. The framework had been torn down and partially put back up again. He should have been happy at his progress, he thought, glancing around, but he knew how quickly it could be destroyed.

By fire.

Fire destroyed lives, property, and memories all in one hot, burning flash.

So, what did he expect to find in the little town of Faith? Faith? He almost laughed at the stupidity of his joke. Was it peace for his soul, answers for his guilt-ridden questions, or a vulnerable woman with sexy green eyes and a body to match?

He was nothing but a sinner. Did he think she could lead him to everlasting salvation?

Or was he the one to lead her?

The thoughts scared him.

He didn't want to think much about his motive for offering to help her. He told himself helping Jade was simply therapy, a way to make up for the past, for what had happened to the other mother and son. It was a way to try to rid himself of his ghosts.

But since he'd spoken with Jade the night before, he'd realized he needed to keep things simple. He'd all but told her he'd marry her himself, but really he wasn't ready for any commitments, and he couldn't have a platonic marriage with someone like her.

He took a deep breath, reassuring himself he had nothing to worry about. Jade would never take him up on his offer.

The warm night breeze whistled through the ponderosa pines, bringing the scent of evergreen . . . and something else. Something sweet.

He turned and saw Jade standing in the doorway. For a moment they just stared at each other, then he saw her draw in a deep breath and nod at the flower box in his hands.

"That's beautiful," she said.

"Thanks." He carefully set the box down before he dropped it. "Let's hope Mrs. Jacoby agrees with you."

"Could I ask you something?" she said, walking toward him.

Decisiveness was written all over her body, from the determined expression on her delicate face to her bold stride. She had something on her mind.

"Sure."

As he pulled up a couple of folding chairs, he studied her face, her eyes, her mouth, all the while wondering why his heart was pounding and his breathing was labored.

Was it because of the fact that lately she blushed whenever they were together, or that he knew what was troubling her and the protective urges he felt every time she was near were getting harder and harder to ignore?

"This isn't easy for me," she said.

He watched as she gathered her hair up with her fingers, pushing the thick strands off her shoulders and letting them drop.

He waited until she settled in a chair and then followed suit, sitting next to her.

"I've been getting some letters from my ex-husband, Rick. He wants to see his son. He wants his son, is more like it."

His gaze followed her profile to the curve of her mouth as she talked. Red, cherry, ripe. He swallowed. "Has Lucas seen him yet?"

"No." She practically shouted the word, then quickly looked around the empty addition as though she didn't want Aunt Ruth to know she was out there, alone, talking to him. "Rick hasn't cared to see his son until now."

"Does Lucas want to see his father?"

"I don't know. I haven't asked him."

"Do you think it's fair to Lucas to keep him in the dark?"

She squeezed her fingers together. "The only thing he understands is what he has now, with me and Aunt Ruth. All the more reason why I can't allow his father to take him away."

"You sound like you're stuck," he said, feeling a growing concern for Lucas's welfare as well as hers.

With the tip of her foot, she toyed with the few small bristle cones that had fallen from the pines overhead, through the open beams of the roof. "I am. You see, I declared personal bankruptcy two years ago. Aunt Ruth and I were having trouble keeping the business going, but despite that setback, I have been doing all right for myself and Lucas."

"A lot of people have had similar problems and manage to get back up and running."

She nodded. "I know. But I'm afraid Rick will use that against me to show that I can't take care of Lucas. Like I was a bad mother or something."

"That sounds like a stretch. You seem to be a good mother."

She looked up at him. "I know it may sound stupid to you, but I can't take any chances or ignore any crazy reason that Rick might come up with to use against me."

Leaning his elbows on his knees, he stared out into the thicket of mountain laurel and shrubs beyond the framework of the addition, though he saw nothing but darkness.

He kept telling himself he wasn't interested in her, but he was. She was a compassionate, appealing, and sexy-looking woman.

If he wasn't mistaken, she was interested in him too. He'd seen the signals of desire in women before and he'd swear he'd seen that look from Jade.

"That's why," she went on, "I've thought about what you said yesterday."

He glanced at her, and all he saw were her big eyes, the trembling of her mouth, and the soft wave of her hair falling over her shoulders.

The thick tension between them stretched like a live wire.

"Want to be more specific?"

She hesitated for a moment. "Do you regret anything you said last night at Sue's?"

"No. My word is my bond."

"Okay. Remember how we talked about my immediate problem?" Her voice dropped to a low pitch as though she was embarrassed. "If Rick somehow shows the courts that I still can't manage my finances, that's just one more point in his favor. I can't let that happen, though I don't know how to stop him."

"I see that your ex is going to be hard to handle, isn't he?"

"That's definitely an understatement."

"So what's your next move?"

"You know what my attorney has told me," she said. "What he's told me from the beginning. I need a husband."

Trace felt his heartbeat speed up. Without thinking, he grasped her hands in his. To his surprise she didn't pull away.

"I've never really trusted anyone before," she said. "Except Aunt Ruth. Certainly not a man."

She leveled her gaze with his.

He couldn't let go of her, his hold tightening little by little. He didn't know why, except a voice deep inside him told him to hang on. He didn't want to let go of her, and her gaze told him she felt the same.

"I've never met anyone like you," she said, her voice faltering. "Something tells me I can trust you. And I don't understand why."

"Jade, what are you saying?"

She paused, looking away for a moment, staring at nothing.

The silence tore at him.

"Help me, Trace," she said, her voice no louder than a whisper. "Help me find a husband."

FOUR

He touched her.

He was temptation and salvation, and he scared Jade beyond reason. He was wonderfully handsome, unspeakably sexy, but could he help her and Lucas? Would he ask her to marry him? Could he be the hero she'd been waiting for, or would he break her heart?

Her palms turned moist, and her heart pounded so hard, she could hear the erratic beat in her ears.

"I know it sounds crazy," she said. "A woman asking another man to help her find a husband. I feel kind of awkward asking."

"I offered my help and I meant it."

"I'm relieved you said that. I think I'm going out of my mind with this whole thing."

He released her hands, and she suddenly felt cold. Leaning back in his chair, he stared so intently at her, her anxiety level shot up toward the stars.

Maybe he was regretting his offer, she thought. She couldn't tell. They had known each other for such a short time. That made her plea for help all the more crazy. She twined her fingers together.

"Helping people is a habit of mine." He grabbed her hands again and forced her fingers to relax.

"I'm glad to hear that," she said, "though I'm curious. Why would you want to help me?"

"I admire you for taking control of your life."

She was surprised at his statement. He saw something in her that sometimes she couldn't see herself. Though she had to admit that despite the struggles to make her own decisions and raise Lucas, she'd done reasonably well. "Some people call that stubbornness."

"Perhaps."

"Have you ever been in love? I mean truly in love."

"Once. But my life is different now."

"Oh? How's that?"

She knew she shouldn't ask any more questions, but she couldn't stop herself. She wanted to know more about him and what his life had been like before he arrived in Faith.

"I like the slow, simple pace of this town," he said.

She struggled not to smile, realizing that *she* was beginning to like the deep, quiet sound of his voice.

"I also like the quiet and private life that I have right now."

Their casual conversation seemed to have relaxed

him a little, but it had the opposite effect on her. She forced herself to focus on what he was saying instead of on his soft, rumbling voice and sensual mouth.

"I don't know exactly how I'd go about doing this," he said. "It's not like I know a lot of eligible bachelors here in town. So, what would you be looking for in a husband?"

A rush of heat flamed up her cheeks as she realized what he'd just said. How could she have misunderstood his intentions? How could she have been so stupid as to think that he wanted to marry her? She struggled to find her voice. "Ah, I don't know."

"Give me a quick rundown. Nothing specific. We can fine-tune the process as we go along. I just need to get some ideas of who the right guy might be."

She stared at him, feeling a sick wave go through her stomach. "You—you want to discuss this now?" she asked around the suffocating tightness in her throat. "Seriously?"

"Sure. I know you're in a hurry. Do you want to back out?"

She wanted to scream her frustration. "I can't. My ex will be breathing down my neck before I know it. I have to do this."

"All right," he said. "Let's get back to my original question."

"I don't really know what I'm looking for in a husband." She shifted in her seat to get a better look at him, waiting for him to say something different. That perhaps he'd be the best husband.

Instead, he simply watched her. The sounds of

the pine needles whispering in the night breeze grated on her nerves.

She felt trapped by his stare, and disturbed by the thrill it brought to her. She thought about running into the safety of the house, but that would be cowardly. She had to face whatever was coming, no matter how humiliating.

"You have to know something of what you desire in a man," he said.

She swallowed hard as she stared at his mouth, realizing it was becoming a habit of hers. She knew his line of questioning was getting downright risky, and she was being too careless with her runaway emotions.

"Ah . . . he has to be kind and understanding," she said, searching for the right words and her lost composure. "Especially where my son is concerned, though as I said before, Lucas will not know the details. I won't consider it a real marriage, so my 'husband' will have to understand that we will not consummate this relationship."

"No sex?"

"Of course not."

She shifted her gaze to stare at her toes peeking out from her sandals.

"Hmm," he said, causing her to look up at him. A slight smile creased his lips. "No sex. That definitely puts a hitch in my search."

She could feel the heat of embarrassment crawl up her cheeks. "This is only for a short while, until the courts decide in my favor for full custody of Lucas," she said, ignoring his last statement. "Then I would get an annulment."

"Jade," he said, his voice barely a murmur above the rustling leaves that scattered across the concrete foundation. "What are you really looking for? A man to love? A man to love you back? It's possible, you know."

She froze. His words were like a flame rippling over her raw, exposed nerves. She shook her head. "No, it's not. There's no such thing except in little-girl daydreams. And I'm not a little girl anymore."

"That's right. You told me before that you've sworn off men."

"Jade darlin', are you out there?" Aunt Ruth called from inside the house.

"Yes, Aunt Ruth."

"Lucas is waiting to say good night."

"I better get going," Trace said, and stood.

He placed a warm hand on her shoulder, then brushed aside a lock of her hair.

She shivered. The words she wanted to say were forever lost on her lips.

"I'll think about what we talked about," he said. "I'll see you tomorrow."

"But it's Saturday. You don't work weekends."

"I know. Sleep tight."

Before she could utter another word, he left.

The streets were unusually crowded for a warm Saturday afternoon, with people cluttering the sidewalks and cars fighting for any available parking space underneath the aspen and willow trees lining Main Street.

Summer tourists, Trace thought. Had to be.

He took in a deep breath of the evergreen-scented air. Hot and dry. Ready and ripe for fires, he noted as he walked out of Ike's Bar and Grill and stood on the sidewalk to look around.

He could hear children's laughter as they played in a nearby park and bits of conversation from strolling couples passing along the sidewalk. A few people waved in recognition, and he waved back.

His stomach twisted, reminding him that his hurried lunch of a chiliburger and a plateful of steak fries, plus one beer, was not something he should indulge in on a regular basis. Nor was listening to the constant blaring of Aerosmith mixed with Garth Brooks on Ike's jukebox. Both artists were good in their own way, but not one right after the other after the other.

Plus he didn't want to admit that his upset stomach could be a result of Tamara Wilkes's unwanted attention or the fact that the list of eligible bachelors he'd jammed into his rear pocket was filled with names of men he was hoping Jade would reject on the spot.

They were certainly men he'd reject on the spot.

This was nuts, he thought, pulling out the list to read it once more. He'd deliberately, along with the help of Ike and Tamara, compiled a list of dull guys and boorish jerks.

Mike Carlton? Trace nodded in silent approval.

Mike was too much into hunting and fly-fishing to interest Jade. Though Lucas could learn a little about outdoor sports.

Trace's gaze dropped down to the second name. Tim Fletcher. Recently divorced from his second wife, Tim was a slob, though he could provide very nicely for Jade and Lucas with the income he hauled in from his booming video store.

Dave Barnstrom was third on the list and a player, at least according to Tamara.

And she would know, Trace decided with a grin. And Hal Reyes? Trace paused, then shoved the list back into his pocket. Hal Reyes was plain too old.

The list was a gem, he thought. But that was the plan. And as much as he tried to deny it, no man was going to be a good enough husband for Jade. Even a temporary one.

"Trace, honey," Tamara called.

He turned to see the saucy, auburn-haired woman stroll out of the restaurant. She wore a white T-shirt with IKE'S BAR AND GRILL emblazoned on it in red letters, tiny black shorts, and red-and-black cowboy boots. She walked up to him and hooked her arm through his.

"Watcha doin' tonight?" she asked, her voice dropping to a sultry purr.

He smiled at her. No doubt about it, Tamara was a looker, with long silky hair and satiny skin that begged to be touched. At any other time in his life, she would have been the perfect distraction to while away the lonely nights.

"Oh, I don't know," he said, letting his gaze travel over the low-cut V-neck T-shirt and abbreviated shorts she wore.

He was a man, after all, and he could be tempted from time to time. But not now, he realized. Tamara reminded him too much of his ex-fiancée, Valerie. Considering how complicated his life was right now, Tamara would just have to wait for another time.

It was easier that way.

If only he could apply that same logic to Jade. Because the longer he stayed around her and wrapped himself up in her predicament, the more difficult it would be to walk away.

And walking away was exactly what he planned on doing as soon as he completed the job at the bakery. He didn't need the complications that would come with a marriage and a ready-made family. No sense in adding more problems to his life. He had enough right now, even though he was, through a lot of determination, solving them.

His last telephone call with his father, a couple of nights earlier, confirmed that. Talking freely with his father was a good sign that he was getting on with his life. With each conversation, he felt their relationship improving and growing stronger, returning to what it had been. Most important, he knew he needed to try again to be a firefighter.

"Well, come on, honey," Tamara said, pulling him back to the present. "What's up for tonight?"

"Maybe I'll take in a movie on Sue's cable or read a book."

"Now, that sounds downright boring," she said, running a bright pink fingernail up his bare forearm. "I could think of something far more interesting to do than read some dumb ol' book. Right there in that cozy room you have at Sue's."

Trace moved away enough to give himself some breathing space, yet not so much as to appear as impatient as he felt. "I bet you do. And I'll keep that in mind. But in the meantime my cousin doesn't approve of extra guests at her B and B."

"Well, honey, when are you goin' to move out and get your own place, then?"

"I don't know," he said as he thought about the Dryer cabin. Faith was a great little town for a brief getaway, but to live here permanently? To his surprise, he could picture Jade living at the cabin as easily as he pictured himself.

"There's a dance here tonight at Ike's." Tamara's voice broke into his fantasies. "It's gonna be a warm-up celebration for the up-and-coming Jubilee Days we have here in town this month."

"I don't know how to dance."

"Don't worry about it, honey, you don't have to. You can follow my lead." She rubbed her palm against his chest. "You know, just press that muscular body of yours against mine." She smiled a pretty smile at him. "I won't lead you astray. I promise."

"I'll see what I can do," he said, taking her hand in his and squeezing it.

He glanced down the street, looking for an excuse to get away from the woman, and he saw Jade.

He frowned. And who was she with? Not anyone he recognized.

A tall blond-haired man had stepped out of a small sporty car and stopped Jade as she walked along the sidewalk. They started to talk in what appeared to be an instant argument.

Watching the exchange, Trace felt a prickly itch crawl up his back and rest at the base of his neck. Behind him, Tamara was saying something, but he couldn't quite hear her.

The man wrapped his arms around Jade's shoulders and pulled her to him. Jade shoved him back.

The act made Trace's skin positively crawl and his heart thump wildly.

"Excuse me, Tamara," he said. "I'll see you later."

"Don't forget, Trace honey. Tonight at Ike's," she called after him. "I'll be here, waitin' for ya."

He mumbled something under his breath, his focus on the man with Jade. A strange protective urge seethed inside him, and he found his hands clenching at his sides.

The man shouted an obscenity at Jade and waved his fist, then he turned and marched to his car. Within seconds the small import shot down the street, scattering tourists toward the safety of the sidewalks.

Jade turned and headed in the opposite direction,

toward Trace, her head down. As she approached he could see that she was shaking.

"Hi there," he said when she was a few feet away.

She jerked her head up and let out a gasp of surprise. "Oh, hi. I didn't see you."

"I know. You almost ran into me."

She glanced over her shoulder, then looked up at him. "I guess I should watch where I'm going."

Her voice trembled, and he could see the panic in her eyes. "Who was that?"

"Who? That guy?"

"Yeah." Noticing the red marks on her arms, he gently touched the sore areas. Jade stepped back in what he read as fear.

Suddenly he realized who the man was. And he wanted to break his face.

"Just someone," she said as she nervously glanced down Main Street.

"That was Rick, wasn't it?"

She nodded.

He took her hand and led her to a nearby park bench under some shady aspen trees and away from prying eyes and ears. "Here, sit."

"I, ah, I can't." She pulled away.

"I think we should talk about what's going on."

"I have to get home."

"Okay, I'll drive you."

"No, I have to get home," she said, not hearing a word he said as the panic rose in her voice. Her gaze scanned the park and nearby streets. Anxiously, she looked everywhere and at everyone except him. "I have to see Lucas."

"Jade, listen," he said in a loud voice, snapping her attention to him. "I'll take you home and you can see Lucas. Then we can talk."

"I—I . . ."

He grasped her by the elbow and swung her in the direction of his truck. "I'm taking you home."

Twenty minutes later he pulled into the driveway at the bakery.

Business at the Cinnamon Girl was brisk, but Aunt Ruth took one look at Trace and Jade as they made their way through the store, then she turned to the girl helping behind the counter.

"Shelly darlin'," she said, "take charge here for a few minutes. I'll be right back."

Aunt Ruth followed them down the connecting hall and into the house. "What happened?" she asked the second the door closed behind them.

Trace motioned toward Jade. "She saw Rick."

"Humph. So he's finally shown up." Aunt Ruth pulled Jade into her embrace. "What'd he say, darlin'? Did he do anything?"

"She wouldn't tell me a thing," Trace said.

Jade pulled away from her aunt and rubbed her hands across her face. "Rick said he'd use my bad financial history to show that I would squander Lucas's fortune, and that I wasn't capable enough to take charge of Lucas's trust fund. And, of course, that I'm an unfit mother because I can't make the right decisions for him." She pressed her fingers to her forehead. "I knew he'd do something slimy like that. He's such a greedy jerk. Where's Lucas?"

"He's taking a nap," Aunt Ruth said. "He collapsed after a hard afternoon of playing Marco Polo in Jimmy's pool."

"I'm going up to my room," Jade said, and disappeared up the stairs.

Aunt Ruth turned to Trace. "That man means nothing but trouble."

As much as he hated to admit it, Trace knew he was being sucked into whatever that trouble meant. "Is there anything I can do to help?"

She blew a loose curl out of her face. "I don't know, Trace."

"Name it, Aunt Ruth," he said. In his heart, he knew he had to help somehow, even as logic told him to stay out of a domestic time bomb that was ready to explode.

Aunt Ruth planted her hands on her hips and looked him square in the eyes. "Would you mind staying for a while?"

"Sure. I could stay until dinner."

"No, that's not what I meant. I mean, could you stay overnight?"

His brows furrowed into a frown. "Overnight? Why?"

"I'm afraid that Rick might come and cause a disturbance that could raise hair off a bald man."

"If he does, you call the sheriff."

"I know. But I'd feel much better if you'd stay. I

don't trust that scoundrel. He's liable to do anything."

"I'm not the law."

Aunt Ruth paced the kitchen floor. "You're right. I shouldn't ask something like that when it doesn't involve you." She slumped into a chair and covered her face with her hands. Tiny curls fell over her forehead. "Especially not knowing what you could get yourself into. Not unless you know what kind of creep Rick Kersey is."

"I've already some idea of what a creep the guy is from this afternoon."

Aunt Ruth looked in the direction of the stairs. She rose and closed the kitchen door. "Well, let me amuse you a little more. I think you should know as much as possible."

"Go ahead."

She quickly summarized Jade's relationship with Rick, her pregnancy and how she had come to live in Faith, and Jade's parents.

Trace felt numb with increasing rage as he listened. "Don't worry about a thing, Aunt Ruth," he said, knowing that he might regret what he was about to say. "I'll stay."

"You'll probably scare the pants off him if he decides to show his worthless hide around here." She laughed. "I could pull out the trundle bed in Lucas's room for you."

"Don't trouble yourself, Aunt Ruth. I'll use the couch downstairs."

"I don't mind. And it'd be good for Lucas," she

said, heading toward the bakery. "It'll give him a chance to get to know you better."

"You know, I don't think Lucas—"

Aunt Ruth spun around. "Hmm, what's that, darlin'? Did you say something?"

"Nothing," he said, remembering the red marks on Jade's arms. What difference did it make where he slept? "I can sleep anywhere."

"I know Jade would feel a whole lot better too. With Rick after Lucas, who knows how nasty this can get? I thank you, Trace darlin', from the bottom of my heart."

"I'll stay for as long as you need me, Aunt Ruth."

Now he knew exactly what trouble meant.

"What are you still doing here?" Jade asked from the doorway of Lucas's bedroom a few hours later.

Lucas slid off his bed and came to her side. A video game dangled from one hand and a book in the other. "Trace is gonna stay overnight. He said we could play video games and then he's gonna read with me and sleep in my room."

Her gaze instantly shot across the bedroom to Trace, her heart lurching clear up her throat. She couldn't have him that close, living and sleeping under the same roof with her. It was unthinkable. Her emotions couldn't handle the pressure. And what about Lucas? How would Trace's constant presence affect her son? "He's what?"

Trace rose from the quilt-covered trundle bed

and made his way through the action figures, comic books, and socks scattered across the floor. "It was your aunt's idea."

"That's insane. When did she do that?"

"She pulled out the bed while you were taking your nap," he murmured in her ear, causing the hair along her neck to rise.

"What about Luc—"

"He'll be fine," Trace said before she could finish her sentence. "We're friends."

"A friend that he'd grow more attached to," she whispered. "A friend that could leave."

"He'll be fine."

"You don't know that." Her gaze shot back to her son. "Lucas, stay here and play for a while. I have to talk to Aunt Ruth."

She turned and headed down the stairs. She could hear Trace right behind her. Her aunt couldn't have guessed that having Trace in their home would be enough for her to lose every ounce of composure she had left. She hadn't intended any feelings of desire and need for him to surface, but they had. And what was she going to do with her son?

"Aunt Ruth and I have to discuss this," she said, stopping abruptly at the foot of the stairs.

Trace collided into her and grasped her shoulders to keep from falling over her. His hard chest pressed into her back and he drew in a quick breath.

She glanced over her shoulder at him.

Did he know that his touch was enough to set her oversensitive emotions on fire? Did he know that his closeness was becoming increasingly natural to her, which would make his leaving, as she was sure he would do, all the harder to take?

She eased away from him, hoping he couldn't see that on the inside she felt like shattering. She took a fortifying breath, determined to be strong. Just as she had been in the past.

He followed her into the bakery kitchen.

She quickly glanced around the room, only to see that her aunt was nowhere to be found. She must be out front again.

"You asked for my help," Trace said, "and now you're upset. I'm confused."

She turned to face him and planted her hands on her hips. She wanted to be angry at him. He was just another in a long line of people trying to rule her life. First her parents, then Rick, and now Aunt Ruth and Trace. Somehow, though, she couldn't raise any anger toward him.

"I asked you to help me find a husband," she said, feeling again like a ninny for having seen more in his offer than he'd meant. "I didn't ask you to stay here."

"Your aunt did."

"Are you trying to make me feel like a fool?"

"I didn't think I was. Am I?"

"You're . . ."

"Impossible?" His mouth quirked with amusement.

She slipped into a kitchen chair. "Yes."

He had the ability to see through her every time,

she thought. He was infinitely patient and kind. Definitely inner qualities a husband and father should have. She shouldn't want him, though. She shouldn't care. She wanted to resent him, but she couldn't.

"I thought I was helping," he said.

"I'm sorry." She looked up at him. "You *are* helping, really. I appreciate everything you've done so far. This afternoon has really thrown me."

He pulled up a chair and straddled it backward.

She glanced down at his large hands folded over the edge of the chair and couldn't help but think of other places that he could put them. Not a smart idea, she thought, suddenly blushing.

"Apology accepted."

She cleared her voice and forced an unruffled expression on her face. The last thing she needed was to let him see just how much he affected her.

"It's because Rick showed up today that Aunt Ruth asked you to stay, isn't it?" she asked.

"Uh-huh."

"So you're to be my bodyguard."

"You need one." Reaching out, he touched the spot where the last of the red marks had started to fade, leaving a faint purplish color in its place. "What about your son? What does he need?"

She bristled as goose bumps sprang up her arm. "He needs a father, that much I know. But not Rick."

He moved his chair closer until they were only inches apart. "I know Rick is threatening you. You've got proof right here on your arms. I know he's sent a series of letters too. You should talk with your attorney about getting a restraining order."

She stood and walked toward the kitchen sink. "What good will that do?" She braced her hands on the cool stainless steel, feeling lost and scared.

He rose and followed her, standing so close behind her, she could feel the soft fan of his breath stirring against the bare skin of her neck.

Why had she put her hair up into a ponytail after she rose from her nap? If she'd left her hair down, she wouldn't be feeling his warm breath heating up her already-flaming skin.

Of course, if she'd been smart, she would never have allowed herself to get into this situation with a man like Trace Banyon in the first place.

"A restraining order wouldn't hurt," he said. "At least the police would be on the alert to Rick's potential danger should he decide to get rough again."

"It's a worthless piece of paper. It won't stop him from doing what he wants."

Trace took a deep breath, and she could feel the tension radiating from his body.

"So you do need me and so does Lucas."

She refused to let her emotions take over. She slowly turned around, knowing that admitting that she needed him would only make her more vulnerable. "Really, we can manage. You don't have—"

"Aw, hell, Jade." He moved closer, forcing her to lean against the sink. "I don't believe you."

"What? Are you saying I'm lying?"

He reached out as though to cup her chin, but

drew back before touching her. "Jade," he whispered, his voice much gentler now. "If you want to be stubborn, be stubborn. But don't be stupid too."

She sucked in a deep breath. "I'm not being either."

"Aren't you?"

"I don't like—"

He touched her cheek, his roughened fingertips bringing blasts of heat to incinerate her clear to her soul.

"Jade, you're not thinking clearly."

"What about Rick?"

"What about him?"

"What if he—"

"Does something that's really stupid?"

She nodded.

"I'm not claiming to be some macho tough guy, but at least you have to admit I'd be a formidable deterrent."

She glanced at his muscled arms and broad chest.

"I'm taller than Rick too," he added, as though he knew what she was thinking.

"All right," she said. "I'll see Morris tomorrow and discuss getting a restraining order."

"Good. That makes me happy."

"Well, I'm glad you're happy," she said. Her mind was whirling with confusing thoughts.

"You're not?"

"Happy? Right now? Of course not. I'm scared."

"Then let me tell you the same thing I told Aunt Ruth."

Jade held her breath for what seemed like minutes. She was suddenly aware of the power that emanated from him, strength mixed with the softness and caring she saw in his eyes.

She waited, not moving a muscle. "What did you tell my aunt?"

His hands rested on her shoulders, and she forced herself to remain still.

"I told her I'd stay as long as she needed me."

"But—but what about my say in the matter?"

"Lord, woman, you're stubborn." His eyes glowed a deeper shade of blue. "Then I'll stay as long as *you* need me."

His words rippled over her like a velvet quilt, comforting her, giving her the warmth and security she'd always yearned for.

She was crazy. No, maybe he was right when he said that she was being stubborn and stupid. Because what she was about to say was stupid indeed.

"Stay," she said, feeling her knees just about buckle underneath her. "I want you to stay for as long as it takes to secure Lucas's safety."

FIVE

"Mom?"

Jade shot awake. "What? What, honey? What is it? It's way past midnight."

Lucas crawled up onto her bed. His eyes were wide.

She thought she'd heard something earlier. She'd been worried and scared that maybe Rick would break into the house and take Lucas.

"Trace woke me," Lucas said.

Relieved, Jade put her arms around him and tried to hug him, but he wriggled away.

"You've got to come and talk to him, Mom. He's talking silly stuff. He threw his pillow across the room."

Jade's stomach knotted. She slid out of bed and slipped a lightweight robe over her T-shirt. "What are you talking about? Is he upset at something or what?"

Lucas's eyes grew even wider. "He's sleeping."

Jade took Lucas's hand and started down the hallway toward his room. "But he has to be awake. Are you sure he's sleeping?"

Lucas hitched up his pajama bottoms with his free hand. "Uh-huh. He's sleeping, all right. I know it. I tried to wake him, but he wouldn't budge."

Jade could see the bedroom door was ajar, the room barely lit by a night-light.

She inched closer. She could hear Trace thrashing and turning on the small trundle bed. Her heart sank. He had to be having a nightmare.

"I can't sleep when he does that," Lucas said. "Is he going to do that every night?"

Jade touched Lucas's shoulder. "Remember what I told you? That Trace is staying for a while until he finishes the work on the bakery. That's all."

Lucas rubbed his eyes. "But I can't sleep."

"All right, honey. You go on and sleep in my bed."

"Is Trace gonna be all right?"

"Yes. I think he's having a bad dream, that's all."

"Whatcha gonna do?"

Jade hugged her son. "I don't know. You go on to bed. I'll be right there."

He rubbed his eyes again and yawned. " 'Kay." He turned and walked back to her bedroom.

Now what? Jade wondered. She stared into the semidarkness of Lucas's room, barely able to make out the outline of the large man lying on the bed.

Trace flopped onto his stomach, calling out

unintelligible words. His long legs and arms hung over the sides of the small bed.

She clenched her hands, her nails digging into her palms as she decided what to do.

Taking a deep breath, she pushed open the door. Walking into the room, she could feel Trace's heat, sense the tension and anxiety. He softly cried out again, sending a streak of apprehension rippling up and down her body.

Her heart cried out. She couldn't let this continue. Did she dare wake him? Stop the obvious nightmare he was having?

A few steps from the bed she awkwardly cleared her throat. "Trace, wake up. It's me, Jade."

With a groan, he rolled onto his back.

She stepped closer and could see the sweat inching down his bare chest. His arms and shoulders twitched with each sound.

Longing burst inside her. She had an overwhelming need to comfort him. Leaning over, she touched his shoulder.

His skin was warm and moist, his muscles tight. "Trace," she whispered. "Wake up. You're having a nightmare."

Moaning loudly, he reached out and grabbed her wrist.

Startled, she tried to back up, but he held firm, his fingers pressing into her flesh. In one fast motion, he tugged her toward him until her legs hit the side of the bed.

She slipped to the floor, the soft carpet cushioning her. She didn't pull away. She didn't say a word.

His eyes flashed open.

Her heart skipped a beat.

His gaze locked with hers. She saw the surprise in his face. And something else in his eyes that just about melted her to the spot.

She kept telling herself that she didn't need a man in her life other than a temporary husband.

She didn't need any more complications.

But it was too late.

Trace jerked upright in bed. He'd been having another nightmare.

Or was it a dream?

He stared at Jade, and she stared right back. Her expression didn't change, but he could sense an underlying change in her.

And in him.

Her long raven hair fell over one shoulder. Her robe had parted, revealing the soft skin of her neck above a pale pink T-shirt. The sight of her, with her hair tousled, her eyes still a bit drowsy from sleep, made him want to drag her up onto his lap and kiss the hollow at the base of her neck and taste every inch of her body.

"You were having a nightmare," she said.

He straightened his back, hiding his obvious awareness of her, and leaned against the wall. He ran his hand through his damp hair, welcoming the coolness of the wall against his scarred back.

"Does that mean I'm having a dream now?" he asked.

She tugged on her bottom lip with her teeth. "I don't know. What do you see?"

A vision, he decided, his gaze locking onto her mouth again. Sweet as cherries.

"Just you," he answered.

She drew in a sharp breath.

He glanced down, his fingers still grasping her wrist. He noticed she didn't pull away but instead gazed at him in silent expectation.

"Who are you, Jade O'Donnell? And why did you come into my life?"

"I could ask you the same," she whispered. "Who are you, and are you going to disappear as quickly as you came?"

Her questions shocked him.

He slid his free hand along the back of her neck, reveling in the sudden show of goose bumps along her skin. He grabbed her hair, wrapping the long tresses around his hand. Pulling her toward him until they were a fraction of an inch from each other, he held her head still.

"I can't answer that," he murmured.

"That's too bad," she said in a smoky, soulful voice. "I wish you would. Then there wouldn't be any more confusion between us."

He took in a slow and deep breath, detecting the faint scents of powder and coconut-scented shampoo. "Is that what that is? Confusion? I thought it was more complex . . . like attraction, desire."

"Attraction—"

He concentrated on her eyes and her mouth. The invitation he saw in her eyes was a passionate challenge and hard to resist. He touched her lips with his, then covered her mouth as her eyes slid shut.

Her kiss was surprisingly gentle and it sent his stomach into a wild swirl.

He moved slowly and easily, parting her lips, feeling the delicious sensation race through him. Excitement burned and sizzled between them.

What seemed like a second later, she eased away and drew in a deep breath. Her hands were shaking.

Her lips had been hot and wet and more persuasive than he cared to admit. His own mouth was stinging, burning. All he had wanted was a taste, a small notion of what she was like so he could ignore any further temptations and walk away.

But he couldn't.

Instead, he had a burning desire, an aching need for another kiss.

And another.

She pulled her robe tightly around her waist as she stood. "I . . . ah, I have to check on Lucas," she mumbled breathlessly.

"I'm sorry if I woke him."

"He's all right." She crossed the room and her hand clutched the edge of the door. "He was worried about you. I told you you were having a bad dream."

Damn. How did he explain the nightmares to her, let alone to a child?

She gave him one last look and left the room.

If his nightmares didn't keep Trace tossing and turning at night, then his own foolishness did.

Still several days later he didn't feel much satisfaction in knowing that he'd done the right thing in deciding to help Jade find a husband.

Especially now after the kiss they'd shared.

He wasn't sure he'd done the right thing, either, by staying at the house with Jade, Aunt Ruth, and Lucas.

No one had seen or heard from Rick since the encounter in town. It was as though he had tucked his tail between his legs and run like the rat he was. And though Jade had discussed the matter of a restraining order with her attorney, Trace still felt the need to stay.

But living under the same roof with Jade, plus the emotional connection that was strengthening daily between them, was becoming his biggest problem.

Every moment that he could, he found himself watching her. And every time he heard her husky voice and her soft laughter, he felt the tension heightening between them. He wanted to learn more about her, her moods, her hopes and wishes for the future. He couldn't stop thinking about her.

He looked across the kitchen table to where she sat, looking in her pocket mirror.

"Another date?" he asked.

She nodded. "Dave Barnstrom."

"Oh . . . him."

"You don't have to wait up for me like you did last night. I can manage to unlock the back door myself."

She picked up a skinny tube of lipstick and opened it. With an exact stroke of the creamy-looking substance, she outlined her top lip, then carefully smudged the berry color on her bottom lip.

She glanced in her mirror and tilted her head back to get a better view. She touched her lips together, rubbing and blending the color into a petal-like softness.

Her gaze met his, and he swallowed hard as his heart pounded in his chest. He studied her for a moment while the heat settled all around him.

"I wanted to make sure the door was secure before I went to bed," he said, irritated that he'd gotten so excited watching that sensual lipstick display.

A trickle of sweat ran down his arms. He wanted to press her lips against his. Taste her and feel her once more.

Not smart, Banyon. Not smart at all.

"I have a key," she said.

"Uh-huh."

She frowned at him. "You seem to be a little on edge tonight. How come?"

How come? Because getting any closer to you isn't

smart, that's how come. Because getting involved in your life isn't for me, that's how come.

Before he could answer, Lucas shuffled into the kitchen, his pajama bottoms dragging on the floor.

"Hey, Mom," he said, placing a book on the kitchen table and sitting down. "It's your turn to read."

She groaned. "Oh, Lucas, honey. I forgot. I'm sorry."

"How 'bout now?" he asked.

"I, ah, I—"

"Would I do?" Trace interrupted.

Lucas grinned and slid off his chair, pushing the book across the kitchen table. "Sure. It's all 'bout firemen," he said, flipping the pages. He pointed to a well-worn page. "Right here is where I last read to my mom."

Trace glanced up at Jade and saw a look of appreciation and warmth. She mouthed "thank you" and smiled.

"Remember I told you it's his dream?" she said.

He knew the dreams, the passion, and the excitement of doing a job that he was born to do. "I remember."

Jade turned to Lucas. "Have you brushed your teeth yet? Remember what Dr. Goode said about brushing your teeth."

"I forgot."

She gave him a quick kiss on the cheek. "Go, and when you're finished, I'm sure Trace will read to you."

Lucas turned to Trace. "Is that okay with you?"

"Sure, kid," he said. "But make sure you do an extra-good brush job. All right?"

" 'Kay," Lucas said. With his book securely anchored under his arm, he scurried out of the kitchen.

"I think he likes you," Jade said as she stared after her son.

"He probably likes me better now that he's sleeping in your room and I'm not keeping him awake."

He saw a pink blush spread across her cheeks. No doubt she was remembering, as he was, the kiss they'd shared the other night.

A slight knock resounded on the back door and Sue walked inside. Joining them at the table, she poured herself a glass of lemonade from the pitcher sitting there. "Burrell Construction called again," she said to Trace as she sat down. "They said they'd double whatever you're making now."

"Burrell Construction?" Jade asked, her voice dropping low with concern.

"They're a big construction company in Lake Tahoe," Trace said.

"With an excellent reputation," Sue added. "They're putting up a huge condo complex in Lake Tahoe. And Trace would be a fool not to take it."

"Sue," Trace said, a warning in his voice. "I have a commitment here that I intend to finish."

He could almost hear Jade's sigh of relief from across the table.

"Besides," he continued, "I'm staying around

here until Jade gets married." He leveled his gaze at her and winked when she looked up at him.

Her cheeks flushed a deeper rosy hue, and it was all he could do not to jump out of his chair and pull her into his arms.

A silent warning went off in his head, but it wasn't strong enough to overpower the growing desire he was feeling right then. He told himself he was treading in treacherous waters.

"Oh, that's right," Sue said to Trace. "You're in the matchmaking business now."

Jade gave Trace one of her innocent smiles.

A wave of heat swept through him. Damn, she didn't know what she was doing, he thought, gritting his teeth. "Can someone open a window? It's damned hot in here."

Sue looked puzzled and rose to open the window over the kitchen sink. "What's wrong with you, cousin?"

"Nothing," he lied, pulling the crumpled list of potential husbands out of his pocket. He glanced at Jade. "I suppose now isn't a good time to go over this list again."

"Sure, why not?" she said. "I have a few minutes before Dave Barnstrom picks me up—"

"Trace, you didn't pick him, did you?" Sue interrupted.

Jade nodded. "At least he's the best looking of the bunch."

"God, he's gorgeous, but he's not the marrying kind. You know what I mean?"

Jade didn't answer. She just picked up the pitcher of lemonade and poured herself a glass. "Trace, want some? Your glass is nearly empty."

"Yeah, please," he said, feeling like an idiot. Why had he ever volunteered to help her find a husband?

She reached over and poured a generous amount of lemonade into his glass. The movement brought the sweet scent of cinnamon and some other spice. Her scent.

He breathed deep, knowing how senseless it was to fight the urge to tell her that he, too, didn't like his matchmaking efforts. He wanted to tell her that he didn't want her to go out with Dave Barnstrom, Tim Fletcher, or any other guy on the list.

But he couldn't say a word. He knew she had to do what was best for her and Lucas.

He stared at the list. "Let's see," he said, trying to concentrate. "Last night you went out with Mike Carlton and tonight is Dave Barnstrom. Should I be adding or taking any more names off this list?"

"Let me finish with the list, then I'll let you know how it's going," she said.

"I brought over your mail, Trace," Sue said. She handed him a packet of letters bound together by a rubber band. "One's from your father."

He swallowed his surprise. His father wasn't about to give up on him. "How would you know?"

She didn't laugh or even grin. "You should write him and tell him what happened. He'll understand."

"In fact, I have," Trace said, knowing full well that his secret was now out in the open and that Sue wouldn't let him alone in his effort to patch up his shaky relationship with his father. "I have several times."

"Really, Trace? That's wonderful." Sue leaned her elbows on the kitchen table. "I love Uncle Ty dearly, and he loves you too. I'm so glad you told him."

"I didn't say I told him what had happened. I just said I've talked to him."

Sue blinked. "You didn't tell him about the fire and the accident."

"What fire? What accident?" Jade asked.

"He never told you?" Sue asked Jade.

"No, he didn't," Jade said, looking over at Trace.

"Oops!" Sue shot a worried glance at Trace. "Sorry, cousin."

He pushed aside the stack of letters. "Some other time."

"I suppose," Sue said, "that means you're not going to tell us who you know from the Portland Fire Department? And why they sent you a letter?"

"Boy, who are you tonight?" he asked her. "Sherlock Holmes? What's with all the questions?"

"I didn't know you knew anyone from Portland."

"There's a lot you don't know about me, cousin," he said more harshly than he wanted. "So quit being my mother."

He picked up the letters and flipped through them, searching for a Portland postmark. He was surprised at getting such a quick response. He'd only sent in his application a week ago. He couldn't help but wonder if his father was behind it.

"I'm worried about you," Sue said.

"Don't be."

"Now I'm getting worried too," Jade said.

The vulnerability he heard in her voice knifed through him. Right then, more than anything, he wanted to pull her onto his lap, hold her, and kiss her. The longer he was with her, the stronger was his need to tell her that he was willing to give her more than his protection and his shoulder to cry on.

"Well, I've got to go," Sue said, rising from her chair. "Seems like I've caused enough trouble for one night."

After saying good-bye to his cousin, Trace felt an uneasiness fall between him and Jade.

"I hear Dave's car in the driveway," she said seconds later, and went to the back door.

"Jade," Trace said, coming up behind her.

She stiffened and turned to face him in such a way that their bodies brushed in intimate places he'd just as soon not think about. "Yes?" The word was barely audible.

A thick heavy silence covered the room, and he forced back a groan. She didn't pull away, and her eyes glowed with wonder and eagerness.

The very air around her seemed electrified, and he drank in her nearness, her heat. He could almost feel the softness of her, and his body instantly responded.

"I need to ask you something before you leave,"

he said as he took in every feature of her face, memorizing every lovely detail. He gazed at her upturned nose with the sprinkling of freckles, her thick black lashes shading her green eyes, her luscious, petal-soft mouth.

"Yes," she whispered again. It was as though she didn't want to break the spell between them.

A horn honked.

Trace continued to stare at her. God help him, but he couldn't stop himself. He lifted his hand and trailed his fingers down her cheek, reveling in the velvety softness of her skin. "Maybe you should go."

"No, what were you going to say?" she asked, touching his hand and stopping his fingers at the base of her throat. She held tightly as though she didn't want him to take his hand away.

"It's nothing."

"I want to hear what's on your mind, Trace," she said, her voice weaving its magic around him. "What do you want from me?"

He choked back a groan, fighting against himself. *I want to ask you if you think this list of husbands is such a good idea. Because I don't. Then I want to kiss you, Jade O'Donnell. Again and again until I go crazy wanting you.*

She gazed at him, and her lips parted on a soft sigh. So soft, he barely heard the whispery sound. He could feel his heart and soul being slowly unlocked.

Jade held the key.

Under his fingers, he could feel her pulse beating wildly. Instinctively, he pulled her toward him. He lowered his head close to hers, close enough for him to almost taste, almost feel her trembling lips underneath his.

"This list . . ." he began. "What I mean is . . . ah, what time should Lucas go to bed?"

"Eight. Eight is fine," she murmured. "I don't know. What do you think?"

He moved closer and slid his other hand up into her long hair.

She leaned her head back, her expression filled with a lazy sensuality.

A horn honked again. Longer and more persistent.

He cursed under his breath and stepped back, breaking the warmth between them. "I think you should go." The jerk didn't even have the decency to come to the door. Damn, he thought, feeling tight with need and tight with anger for wanting her so. "I'll take care of Lucas, don't worry."

" 'Night, Trace," she whispered.

Her words sounded so sweet, they brought a chill to his heated skin.

He nodded at her and opened the door.

The effort cost him more than he could imagine as he gently pushed her away from him, out the door, and into Dave's waiting arms.

SIX

Jade felt Trace's presence the minute she opened the door to the addition. She didn't have to see him to know he was there despite the fact that she hadn't seen him for an entire day since her date with Dave.

Even Aunt Ruth didn't know where he'd been.

"It's early," he said, without looking up from the window frame he was fitting. He shut the window and opened it once more. "Couldn't you sleep?"

"I slept fine," she lied.

The truth was she hadn't been able to sleep very well since he'd kissed her the night he had his nightmare.

She glanced at him.

He was wearing his usual worn but well-fitting work clothes. Dusty boots that had seen better days covered his feet. His dark hair was thrown back as if combed in a hurry, and hung in soft waves to the frayed collar of his chambray work shirt.

When had his hair gotten so long?

"Why are you up so early?" he asked.

"I . . . uh . . ." Tension stretched across her shoulders. "I thought I'd jump-start the baking and give Aunt Ruth some extra time to sleep before I made this morning's deliveries."

He looked at her and then returned his attention to his work.

Was he being cool toward her to keep the distance between them? she wondered. Or was he trying to act as though nothing had changed since he'd come to live with them?

Not asking him where he'd been the day before was harder than she thought. There was nothing for her to say, though. It wasn't her place. It wasn't as though they were committed to each other in any way. He could do what he wanted.

A shiver feathered down her spine, and she tried to tell herself that not knowing where he'd been or with whom didn't bother her.

Because it bothered her a lot.

He stood from his kneeling position and checked the window frame one last time. "There. That's finished."

"You've done a beautiful job," she said.

He grunted. "You should pass inspection with no problems. The electrician and plumber did a good job."

"Thanks to you. We appreciate you overseeing all the details."

He walked toward her, a frown between his dark eyebrows. "Have you heard from Rick lately?"

Her stomach tightened as it did every time she thought about her ex-husband. "No," she said. "I believe he went back to San Francisco. Why? Do you want to return to Sue's?"

"No," he said, his frown deepening.

She found herself tracing the fine lines on his face, around his eyes and his mouth, as he spoke. Her gaze dropped down his neck to the wide expanse of his shoulders and chest. He'd rolled up his sleeves, exposing his tanned and muscular arms.

But what was underneath all his muscle and brawn was what drew her. He had a warm and loving heart. He was caring and gentle. More important, he excited her more than any man on their infamous list, more than any man she knew. Period.

"Are you that worried about my ex?" she asked.

"Aren't you?"

She heard the concern in his voice. "I think about him almost every minute," she said. "I lie awake at nights thinking about him."

"I left here kind of suddenly the other night," he said, startling her by bringing up the subject himself. "I thought I'd better explain."

"You don't have to explain anything," she said, biting her bottom lip. "You're free to do whatever you want."

"It was irresponsible for me to up and leave. You don't know what trouble Rick might cause."

She turned her back to him. She didn't want to

hear the softness in his voice as he tried to apologize. She didn't want to see the tender look in his eyes whenever he got too close to her.

"It's okay, Trace," she said, swallowing back her pride. She glanced at him. "Since Morris managed to get that restraining order, I think Rick has seen he's made a big mistake by threatening me like he did that day on Main Street in front of all those people. Though, in reality, that won't stop him from trying to get what he wants."

"I'll take your word for that."

"You can come and go whenever you please," she said, determined to show him how unconcerned she was.

His worn denim jeans stretched across his thighs as he took two steps closer to her. Reaching for her, he brushed a lock of hair behind her ear with his knuckles, sending hot ripples down her back. Warmth spread clear to her stomach as she anticipated his kiss. She wanted him to kiss her. She wanted him to hold her all night.

But despite what she wanted, she couldn't fall for him or his sexy smile and sexy body.

He was hazardous to her emotions, and she needed to keep her mind on what was important. She'd made a mistake once in her life marrying Rick and now was the time to do the right thing.

She tried to step away from him, but he easily took her arm and stopped her.

"Afraid to kiss me again?" he asked.

"I don't think this is a good idea."

"Maybe. Maybe not," he said, his voice dropping low.

She held her breath and counted the extra beats of her racing heart. "All I know is that this isn't part of our arrangement. And you know it too," she whispered.

"Yes," he murmured. His gaze traveled over her face and searched her eyes. "But are you afraid?"

A burning tingling in the pit of her stomach grew hotter and hotter. "A little."

His arms encircled her. He placed one hand at the small of her back and held her firmly to him. "Don't be," he whispered against her cheek.

His kiss feather-touched her with tantalizing persuasion. He skimmed over her mouth, tracing lightly, first her top lip, then her bottom.

His lips and tongue were warm and moist, tasting spicy clean of toothpaste. She could feel the smoothness of his cheek against her face as he pressed harder.

The touch of his mouth on hers sent a shock wave through her entire body. Her knees felt like Jell-O.

She didn't want to want him. She hated him for the feelings he evoked in her. She hated him for taking away that illusion she'd created for herself that she'd finally gained control of her emotions and her life, when he clearly was the one with the control.

She knew she couldn't take a chance of getting

involved and marrying a strong-willed man like Trace. She couldn't revert to her former wimpy self.

Her pulse picked up speed and she breathed deeply, pulling in the scents that belonged to him.

Waves of heat slid down her back, followed by his hands as he tugged her closer to him.

His lips parted hers in a soul-reaching message. He pressed harder, demanding more, and she could feel his body harden underneath the worn denim.

All sanity slipped away and was replaced by a deep swell of desire. Natural responses that she had hidden away for years sprang to life. She tangled her hands in the silky waves of his hair, pulling him against her.

His hands slid lower, over the snug lavender leggings she wore, and tugged at the bottom of her oversized lavender T-shirt. His hands skimmed upward and underneath, touching the bare, heated skin of her rib cage and her back.

"Mommy?"

The squeaky sound of Lucas's voice echoed through the room as loud as a canon blast. And as painfully. She felt as though she'd just been thrown from a moving train.

Trace eased away from her, then walked toward the window he'd been working on earlier.

Dizziness filled her. She slowly turned around to see her son standing in the open doorway. "Sweetie. Why aren't you still in bed? It's early."

Holding his favorite stuffed animal under one arm, Lucas stumbled into the room. With the back of his fist, he rubbed his face and blinked several times. His huge green eyes told her of his confusion. "I couldn't find you."

"Well, I, ah, I've been here with Trace . . . talking." She felt the guilt tighten her throat with each word she spoke.

He shuffled across the concrete floor, his bare feet kicking up fine dust. He stopped in between her and Trace. "Were you kissing my mom?" he asked Trace.

Trace shot a glance at Jade. "Jade?"

Her heart pounded in her chest. She didn't have an explanation. "Yes," she answered truthfully.

Lucas kept his attention on Trace.

"Why?"

Trace knelt in front of the boy. "It's something adults do."

"Why?" Lucas persisted.

Trace glanced at Jade, and she could see a twinkle glow in his eyes.

"It's hard to explain," he said, looking at Lucas again. "Especially so early in the morning, when you should still be in bed sleeping. When you're older you'll understand."

Jade saw her son's wide smile, and her heart sank. She knew then that she'd made a big mistake. Nothing Trace did was wrong in her son's eyes. He was Lucas's hero.

Dismissing the whole affair, Lucas looked up at his mom. "Are you gonna ask Trace if he wants to go with us?"

"I don't know, honey. I told you not to ask about that. Besides, Trace is busy, you know, with his work and everything. He probably isn't interested."

"What's he talking about?" Trace asked.

"Well," she said hesitantly, still feeling the impact of his kiss. "You know the town has been gearing up for weeks now for the summer events. And Lucas wants to know—"

"You want him to come, too, don't you, Mom?"

She gave her son a weak smile. "Yes, honey. Ah, well, we want to know if you wanted to go with us to the Jubilee Days celebration and maybe participate in some of the events."

He gave her a long look, and she thought he had to know how uncomfortable she felt right then. How could he not? She was sure her face was as red as it felt, and the struggle to draw in an even breath had to be equally obvious.

"When is it?" Trace asked.

Lucas held up two fingers. "Two days."

"He's been counting for weeks now," Jade said. "He's so excited."

"It's a lot of fun, right, Lucas?"

"There's lots to do," Lucas said, nodding rapidly. "You can ride horses like real cowboys and pretend you're running from the Indians. Just like the pony riders did, huh, Mom?"

Jade wrapped her arm around Lucas's shoulders and smiled at him. "That's right, honey. The Pony Express days."

"Sounds exciting," Trace said.

She glanced at him. "It starts on Friday and runs for the whole weekend. A sort of big town party."

"And there's the ax contest and you get to win a big prize," Lucas said.

"And what's the prize?" Trace asked.

Lucas giggled and rolled his eyes. He pointed at Jade. "My mom."

"What?"

She shrugged. "Well, not exactly. The winner of the wood-chopping contest gets a basket filled with cinnamon buns. It's our contribution."

"I should have known," he said.

She saw a smile curve Trace's mouth, making her realize that Lucas's enthusiasm had captured his undivided attention.

She held her breath for what seemed like minutes as she waited for his reply. She'd been afraid to ask him to join the Jubilee celebration for fear that he'd say no and break Lucas's heart.

Or was it her heart?

"Okay, Lucas, what do you say?" Trace asked.

Lucas beamed from ear to ear. "I say let's go."

Jade slowly eased her breath out between clenched teeth, waiting for a promise that could be broken.

"Then it's settled," Trace said, and ruffled Lucas's hair. "I'd better sharpen my ax."

Trace lifted the hand trowel filled with the "mud" mixture to seal the seams of the drywall.

With a precise swipe of his spade, he flung the off-white pasty material against the wall and proceeded to seal and cover the seams of the drywall.

The bakery was quiet as well as the house. Jade, Lucas, and Aunt Ruth had gone to early services at church so they would have enough time to spend at the Jubilee Days fair.

Despite the fact that they'd spent part of the last two days at the fair, Lucas didn't seem to have had enough. And despite his own reservations about agreeing to go in the first place, Trace had to admit he'd enjoyed every minute with Jade and Lucas.

He leaned back to check his work. Seeing everything was satisfactory, he sat down in a folding chair to take a small break. Propping his feet on a sawhorse, he watched the early-morning sun peek through the pine trees.

For a moment he let his mind wander as he took in the heavenly scent of evergreen. He still had plenty of time to decide whether or not he'd take the job offer in Portland.

He closed his eyes. How could he go back to fire fighting? What if someone else died because of him? What about that woman and her son, now forever a memory to those who had loved them?

What about the fact that he'd purposely slowed his work on the addition in order to stay with Jade and Lucas—who were haunting reminders of those victims—because he still wanted to make up for the past?

He couldn't change what had happened, but he

could control his future. He could hear again his father telling him that in their last telephone conversation, that he should take the job in Portland. *Get back to what you do best. Face your fears and your demons.*

Well, he'd faced his demons and his fears. He knew that now each time he'd watched Jade interacting with Lucas. It could be a soft touch of her hand on his face, the laughter they shared. He would immediately be reminded that life continued, no matter what. And so would he. His decision was practically made. Except for one major distraction. Jade.

Visions of her danced through his mind as a warm breeze flowed through the open door of the addition, causing the hummingbird wind chimes on the back porch to sing a light melody.

Summer was here. So was the fire season. He could feel it, smell it. It was as though it were a part of him.

"Hey."

Startled from his thoughts, Trace dropped his feet to the floor and sat up.

A slender blond man stood in the open doorway.

Trace stood and automatically reached for his trowel. "The bakery is closed today because of the fair," he said, scooping up more mud.

"I don't care about that," the man said.

Trace smoothed the mixture on the wall before looking at the stranger. His heart raced as recognition settled in his mind.

"Are you Trace Banyon?" Rick Kersey asked.

"Yeah, I'm Trace Banyon," he just about growled. "And I know who you are."

"Good. Then introductions aren't necessary," Rick said, boldly stepping into the room.

Trace looked around, unnerved that anyone could have come upon him without him knowing. He cursed himself for being so careless, especially where Jade's ex-husband was concerned.

"This is hardly a clean place to be," he said. "There's still quite a mess around." He slung more mud onto the wall, managing to drop some onto the cuff of Rick's pants and the tips of his shoes.

Rick raised his eyebrows and caught the towel Trace tossed to him. "I see." He wiped his shoes with a jerky motion. "There's a lot of progress going on in this town. There's money to be made. I wouldn't mind living here someday."

"What can I do for you?" Trace asked, ignoring Rick's attempt at conversation. He doubted the guy had come there for casual chitchat. "You don't look the type who'd like it here. Money or no money."

Rick dropped the towel on the floor. "And just what type do you think I am?"

The guy was handsome. That much Trace had to admit. He could even see Lucas in his father. The same blond hair, the same rakish good looks. But he was sure that was where the similarities ended.

Lucas was sweet and considerate. Like his mother. And Lucas had Jade's eyes.

"There isn't much call for people on the move in this town," he said. His own words startled him.

Wasn't he on the move? Hadn't he told himself life here was temporary? He cleared his throat. "Faith is a small family town."

"You have a sharp eye."

Trace could feel his temper rising, and he forcefully bridled his anger. "What do you want?" he asked, rancor sharpening his voice.

"I'll be blunt. I wanted to see for myself what kind of man would get himself involved in a situation with a woman like Jade."

A knot of anger rose to the top of Trace's throat. He dropped the trowel with a clatter. Mud splashed up his legs and across the concrete floor. He walked toward Rick until they stood face-to-face. "What situation?"

"I want you to know it won't work. This sudden marriage between you and Jade."

"Marriage?"

"Jade's got this shyster lawyer. What's his name? Peterson. This imbecile has her convinced she needs a husband to keep my son from me, but it won't work."

Rich thought *he* was going to marry Jade?

"Whatever she's told you," Rick went on, "is a bunch of you-know-what. So I'm saving you some time, pal. You don't have to marry her. I'm still going to get my son. And that's exactly what I told her other boyfriend, the hardware guy, just before he ran."

Trace was certain he'd never met a more despicable man. The thought of Jade being alone and pregnant with Rick's child roused such a protective feeling in Trace, his anger surged to the fore. Rick must have seen that in his expression, because the smaller man paled and stumbled back a couple of steps.

"Speaking of running," Trace said, jabbing Rick in the chest, "you've got ten seconds to get your sorry-looking butt off this property."

Rick took another step back, snagging his pants on the edge of the sawhorse.

"Or," Trace added, "you and I are going to have it out right here and now."

"You tell Jade I've got the best lawyer in San Francisco," Rick yelled at him. "She shouldn't mess with me and neither should you."

Trace shoved Rick, causing him to lose his balance on the stone walkway that led away from the house and bakery. "I hope you have insurance."

Rick shouted some obscenity over his shoulder and took off.

Knowing he'd scared the jerk should have made Trace smile with satisfaction. But not now. Not when the stakes were so high. Losing Jade and Lucas was definitely too great a risk.

He wanted to laugh at the absurdity of it all. Now he was supposedly getting married.

He watched Rick disappear through the trees and breathed a sigh of relief as he heard a car start and drive off down the street.

He sat in the folding chair and stared at the dry-wall.

Married? That was a crock.

He couldn't get married. Especially to Jade. He couldn't, because that would mean he would have to care. Care even more than he already did. And that was dangerous, because when you cared about something so special and precious, like Jade, it could be gone in a heartbeat.

He stared at his hands. Gone, right through your fingers. Like a puff of smoke.

But what had Jade told Rick?

Either way, he and Jade had to talk.

Morris opened the door of his office to let Jade inside. "I'm glad you got my message. Come on in and sit down."

Jade sat in a leather chair and adjusted her long calico skirt. "Will this take long? Lucas is waiting in the car to go to the fair." She smiled. She couldn't remember seeing her son quite so happy as he'd been in the last couple of days.

"Not too long," Morris said. "I got a call from Laura Sagebarth in San Francisco."

"Who's she?"

"Rick's attorney."

"Great," Jade muttered. "Here we go."

"Why didn't you tell me Rick was an accountant?"

Surprise widened her eyes. "I didn't know what he's been doing lately."

"If Rick wins joint custody, his next move is stepping right into being appointed as trustee in Thorton Stevens's place. Rick has the experience in money management, and that looks good to a judge. As joint custodian, he can easily tap into Lucas's inheritance."

Jade struggled to catch her breath. "So that's what he's up to. That's how he plans to get the money." She met Morris's stare. "My chances of being appointed are—"

"As I've told you before, they're not good. With your bankruptcy and the lawsuit Spencer Towns had recently brought, it doesn't look good."

"We're making payments to Spencer."

"I understand."

"Now what?"

"It still might appear that you wouldn't be able to handle Lucas's trust." He leaned back in his chair. "We have a ticking bomb here, Jade."

"I know."

Morris tapped his fingers on his desk. "So when are you getting married?"

She let out a weary sigh. "It's not when, but to whom."

"See those old carriages and buggies along the wooden sidewalks?" Jade asked.

Startled from his thoughts by the sound of her husky voice, Trace stopped counting the change he held in his hand. He handed Lucas a couple of quarters and glanced across the street where several buggies and an old Wells Fargo stagecoach were lined up.

"We're in the older section of town where several old buildings have been preserved," Jade went on, pointing across the street as though he were a tourist visiting for the first time. "Including the hotel, which first opened in 1864, and the old jailhouse, which is now a museum."

"Mommm," Lucas groaned. He pulled on the hem of the white apron that covered the front of her calico dress and let out an exasperated sigh. "We know. Me and Trace helped put up the stuff, you know."

Trace grinned at her. "You're talking to a pro here, Jade. You should have seen him work."

She tried to laugh. "I'm sorry, Lucas. My mind is elsewhere. I guess I forgot."

"Trace took his hammer and pounded those nails in, and I followed him and helped hang all those red, white, and blue banners over the front of the booths," Lucas said loudly, the pride clear in his voice.

"You did a great job, kid," Trace said, remembering how the work during the day before the fair had been an easy excuse to try to block out the thoughts of Jade, but also had created a closer bond between him and Lucas.

He shot a look in Jade's direction. Since her short visit with Morris earlier that morning, he had grown concerned about her. Something had to be bothering her, which made finding the right time for them to have a talk all the more imperative.

The more he started to care about her, the more he realized it wasn't working. He didn't want any of this to happen, but circumstances seemed to keep throwing him in Jade's direction.

"Mom, Mom," Lucas said. "Trace gave me some money. Can I get some cotton candy?"

She glanced at Trace. "You would have to do that."

He shrugged. "It's only this time."

"That's what you said yesterday about the ice cream and corn dogs."

He smiled. "One more day to go a little crazy. That's what being a kid is all about."

"Were you crazy as a kid?"

"Insanely so."

"All right," she said to Lucas, who was halfway to the candy booth before she finished speaking, waving wildly as he caught up with Aunt Ruth.

"You're so good with him," she said softly to Trace.

"It's easy. You've done a terrific job raising him, Jade. You should be proud."

"I am." She watched her son walk across the park with her aunt, cotton candy in hand.

"It must have been hard raising him alone."

She walked with him to a shady stand of aspen trees where they'd previously spread a blanket on the thick grass to eat their lunch. The location gave them a perfect view of most of the booths and activities.

"Sometimes," she said. She sat down and pulled her dress over her knees. "There were times I wished Lucas had a father, but I knew that Rick wasn't the answer. It was a mistake to marry Rick, but not to have Lucas."

"He's a great kid."

"My aunt has been a tremendous help. And so have you, Trace. I want you to know I appreciate all you're doing."

He gave a slight smile, but didn't feel so happy about it. He popped open a can of soda as he tried to think of a good way to begin their talk. "When's your next court date?"

"Oh," she said, her voice faltering. "I guess I forgot to tell you."

He sat down next to her. He could hear the anxiety piercing her voice.

She pulled a small date book out of her purse. "Morris got a continuance." She flipped the pages. "Nine-thirty on August thirteenth."

"I'll be there."

"Wouldn't you know it?" she said, shoving the book back into her purse. "Just my luck."

"What?"

"It's a Friday."

"You must be superstitious."

She leveled her gaze at him. "Just worried."

"You must love Lucas a lot to worry like you do."

"From day one. And when anything involves my

ex, I have good reason to worry even more." She looked down at her hands, clasped in her lap. "Here I thought I'd found someone who'd love me for what I was, and not for the money my parents had, or the social status. Just me and my . . ."

She let her voice trail off as though she was in deep thought. "Do you have any regrets?" she asked after a few silent seconds.

"About . . . what?"

"Getting involved with my crazy family?"

He touched her chin, drawing her attention. What could he tell her? That she was the only decent thing in his life at the moment and that he wasn't sure what he would do if she weren't there? That despite his determination to stay away, he was being drawn closer?

"No," he answered.

"Because I feel like such a fool," she said. A tear slid down her cheek and she quickly wiped it away, but not before he noticed.

Wariness warned him against pulling her into his arms and soothing away all her pains. She valiantly held on to her composure and her tears. She seemed determined not to let another tear go unchecked.

"You're not foolish," he said.

"Oh, yeah?"

He could hear the defensiveness in her voice. "I've been around you long enough to see for myself."

She sniffled loudly, then cracked an inane joke to

hide her uneasiness. He didn't know how she managed to continually warm his heart. But she did.

"I think we've all been through some pain or another," he said. "My mother died when I was very young. I don't remember her well."

"I'm sorry to hear that," she said, her voice taking on a softer tone. "Really I am."

"I loved her very much. I know that she loved me too."

"When I was younger, I tried to convince myself that just because my parents were never around didn't mean they didn't love me."

"So you married Rick as fast as you could?"

"I've done a lot of stupid things in my life," she said, wiping the corners of her eyes.

Against his better judgment, he took her by the shoulders and pulled her to him. To his surprise, she allowed him to hold her. "Go on and cry if you want. You don't always have to be so strong."

"Just stubborn," she said, and sniffled again as she pressed her cheek against his chest.

He smiled and skimmed his lips along her hair, kissing lightly. He breathed deep of the coconut-shampoo scent. "Stubborn? Okay, I'll agree with you on that one."

He closed his eyes for a moment, holding her in his arms. She didn't pull away, but instead snuggled deeper into his embrace.

The noises from the crowds seemed to disappear. It was as though they were wrapped in their own private cocoon. Second by second all he could hear was the pounding of his heart and her steady breathing.

He couldn't say no, Jade thought. Especially after she'd told Rick that lie. And boy, was it a big one. She was determined to get what she needed. What she needed for Lucas.

And that was a father.

Now was the perfect time.

She swore she wouldn't be a pushover. Not now. Not like the many times when Rick had made her feel so inadequate and ugly. She'd come far since Lucas was born, and she realized she was strong. But right now she had to be stronger than she'd ever been. She had to convince Trace. He liked Lucas and he'd helped her so much already.

The air felt warm and thick, heavy with the scent of evergreen and wild peach blossoms. She leaned away from him, and he shifted his weight against an aspen tree. She noticed the disappointed look on his face and didn't miss the deep breath he took.

What a mess. She hadn't wanted to tell Rick that lie about her marrying Trace, but it was necessary to protect Lucas. "I'm not disturbing you, am I?"

"You always disturb me," he said in a low, husky voice that sent tingles up her back.

"I've given you a lot of trouble, haven't I?"

He frowned. "Gee, I don't know why you'd say that. Though I should have known after I got hit with that cold blast of water that morning that there'd be plenty of trouble to go around."

Yes, she was insane, all right, she thought, feeling as if her heart would explode right out of her chest. It didn't matter when she asked him or how she asked him. It had to be done and now was as good a time as any. Their lives wouldn't change that much, she rationalized. They would continue to live in the same house, continue the closeness, the intimacy of a real family.

Only the real-family part wasn't real.

"Trace, I have no shame, no pride left," she said after a moment. Her voice shook, and her breath seemed to freeze in her lungs. "All I have in my life is my son. Just love for my son."

"I know you do."

His voice was soft and gentle. Just as it was every time she talked about her son.

"You like Lucas, don't you, Trace?"

"Yeah. I told you. I think he's a great kid."

"He likes you, too, you know," she said, looking into his deep blue eyes.

Her heart seemed to falter in her chest. She felt as though she were moving in slow motion. "He sees you as his hero."

"Jade, don't say that. I'm nobody's hero."

But you are, she thought.

"Trace, this is hard for me. But . . ."

Coward. The word roared in her ears.

"But what?"

"Trace, will you marry me?"

SEVEN

He simply stared at her.

"Um, Trace . . . you have a terrified look on your face," Jade said.

He told himself that he didn't want to get married, that he really wanted to be left alone.

"Married?" he repeated.

Her words stunned him despite the hints Rick had dropped a few hours earlier. He didn't know what to say. He didn't know what to think about the sudden turn of events.

"Yes, married."

All he could think about was how he wanted to crush her in his embrace, breathe deep of her perfume, and give her all the comfort he could.

But marriage? Wasn't that taking it a little too far?

Her dark hair shimmered in the afternoon sun,

making his fingers itch to stroke the glossy tresses that fell in soft waves across her shoulders.

"You're not expecting us to fall in love, are you?"

"Marriage and love don't always go hand in hand," she said, her voice sounding rough and disappointed. She laughed nervously as she stood and began to pace in front of him. "I mean, it would be ridiculous for us to even think that we'd fall in love."

Yeah, right, fall in love, he thought. How ridiculous.

She turned to meet his gaze. Her eyes were large and pleading.

She needed his help once more.

"Trace," she said, her voice sounding desperate. "All I need is time. Time to get through the court dates, time to close the books on this forever. And as I've said before, this is temporary. Lucas won't even know that we're technically married. You won't have to become his stepfather or anything like that."

A twinge of resentment shot through him. Why should he care whether or not she told Lucas? he wondered. Jade's refusal to reveal the marriage to her son only made it more apparent that she wouldn't consider it a real marriage either.

But maybe he needed her help, too, he reasoned.

It didn't take much to see that life would be a heck of a lot easier for him if he were a married man. If he did marry her, and if he stayed married until she got full custody of Lucas, it would keep women like Tamara Wilkes at bay.

Jade would become his insurance policy.

Lucas's welfare entered his mind. He didn't want to see Rick win custody of the boy, either. To put it mildly, the man didn't seem the fatherly type.

So maybe getting married wasn't a bad idea.

If they could manage to keep their emotions out of it and stick to the business deal that it was.

His jaw clenched. "This is an interesting request. And a surprise."

"But honest."

He smiled to himself, enjoying how her assertiveness showed itself every time she tried to protect Lucas.

"I don't care about myself," she added.

"You should."

"I don't want you to take this wrong, and it's not that I'm not concerned about you, but Lucas has to come first."

"I know," he said, respecting her for her courage and love for her son.

He felt careless and foolhardy himself, but he didn't care. What did he have to lose at this point? Besides his heart? He stood, moving close to her, and felt the heat between them instantly flare. He took in her subtle perfume, liking it more with each breath.

Forcing himself to concentrate, he looked into her eyes, refusing to let his gaze drop to her petal-soft mouth. If he let his mind slip even once, he knew he'd do something that was liable to embarrass them both.

"So you want to marry me?"

He could see the tension in her jaw. "Do you

mind me asking what happened to the names on the list? What about them?"

"You're joking, of course. Because every name on that list was a joke."

He grinned. "I thought the list was filled with—"

"Losers." She settled back on the blanket, her gaze fixed on something going on at the fair.

Didn't she realize there were hidden feelings between them waiting to be discovered? And if discovered, they could be dangerous and complicated far beyond what either of them could imagine? Especially if they got out of control?

Was she willing to risk that?

Was he?

These were issues neither one of them could avoid. At least he couldn't, he argued with himself as the thoughts raged through him.

But Jade and Lucas had managed to break through his locked-up heart and soul when no one else had.

"Kit decided he didn't want to see me anymore," she said a few seconds later, brushing her hair aside with the back of her hand. "And the rest, I'd rather not even comment on."

The tone of her voice told him she was embarrassed.

Secretly, he was glad Kit had turned out to be the coward that he was, and the others, well, any questions concerning them were better left unanswered. "I wouldn't be worried about them. Kit isn't good enough for you. Or the rest of them, either."

"You did this on purpose."

He shrugged. "I know that Rick scared the hell out of Kit."

She turned to him. "How did you know?"

He gritted his teeth when he saw the panic flaring in her eyes. "Actually, Rick showed up while everyone was at church."

"Which Sunday?"

"Today."

She moaned in frustration, and her cheeks flushed a faint red. "I don't know what else to do," she said. "It's only for a short while, Trace, then I swear you can leave and get on with your life. I just can't lose my son."

The desperate sound of her voice, her vulnerability, tore at him.

"I know you don't need any more complications than I do," she said.

He nodded. "You're right. I don't need a lover in my life."

"But I have to save my son. So how much worse could it get?"

A lot, he thought. "Well, I'm glad that's out in the open."

"We have to be completely honest."

"I agree. I don't want anything permanent."

"Neither do I." After a few seconds of tense silence she added, "Trace, I need your help. If you don't marry me, Rick will take Lucas. I don't have much money to fight him."

Her words came out in a bare whisper.

Trace's heart pounded hard. "Jade, look at me."

He knew her proposal wasn't anything more than an attempt at self-preservation. Or his accepting her proposal, either. He shouldn't be sympathetic. He should stop while he was ahead.

But for some strange reason, he couldn't. For once, he ignored the warning in his heart. His gaze caught hers and held. "When is our wedding?"

The past six days had been the longest days of her twenty-eight years, Jade thought. Her anxiety had settled in when she'd realized that, yes, she was getting married again.

And Trace was to be her husband.

The stress of pulling together all the details of a hastily planned wedding and interacting with Trace while he finished working in the bakery had affected her more than arriving in Faith, pregnant and divorced, had done. But becoming a married woman again, in a loveless marriage, was one memory that would stay with her forever.

As the week passed and her wedding day drew closer, she kept asking herself if she'd made the right decision.

When she wasn't plagued by those thoughts, she had plenty to keep her busy. By the end of the week, she had barely enough time to pick up her marriage license at the El Dorado County Courthouse, order a modest bouquet, and find the right dress.

Luckily for her, Aunt Ruth had taken care of the

wedding cake and decorations. Sue had handled all the dinner preparations, and her attorney had arranged to squeeze the Saturday date onto Judge Howard Desmond's schedule, which had been nothing short of a miracle.

She had briefly considered holding the wedding at one of the small intimate chapels surrounding Lake Tahoe. The ceremony, however, was only a formal legal detail that would take a matter of minutes. Still, she couldn't help but think how nice it'd be if she had her wedding at the Fantasy Inn or the Lakeland Village Resort.

Jade checked her reflection in the large mirror that hung in the ladies room at City Hall. Her pale face and huge green eyes stared back at her. She tried to smile but couldn't. She couldn't help but think that she looked more like a scared doe than a blushing bride on her wedding day.

"Please, God, let him show," she said aloud.

"You say something, darlin'?" Aunt Ruth asked from the doorway. "The judge is ready."

Jade whirled around to face her aunt. "Oh. It's time already?"

"Yes, darlin'. It's your big moment."

"Ah, my big moment."

"Most brides are filled with excitement and anticipation for their big day and big night," Aunt Ruth said, walking toward her. "I understand your hesitation, but try to make the best of this."

"My only excitement is that I have a chance of keeping my son."

"That's what's called reality and life. Not some fairy tale, Jade."

"I know. I've been the blushing bride once before."

"But not as beautiful as you are now."

She realized her aunt was being kind, as usual, but it still didn't help her nerves. "I know Trace is doing me a favor I can never repay. I owe him so much, and I don't know where or how to begin to express my gratitude."

"He doesn't expect much, darlin'. Just be your sweet self and everything will be fine."

Would he expect sex in exchange, even after the conversation they'd had about that subject? She had to admit the idea of having sex with Trace was tempting and tantalizing. She had the same feelings as other women, feelings she'd tried to ignore. He was a handsome man, and sexy.

But, she thought with a new determination, she ruled her own body, not the other way around. She knew the power sex had over people, and she didn't want to fall under anyone's spell.

Especially Trace's.

It would only mean there'd be more closeness between them.

Jade checked the mirror one last time, hoping to see a change in her face. She saw none.

She wanted to feel happy and excited, but fright had taken up residence instead. She picked up her hip-length ivory jacket and slipped it over her sleeveless ivory-and-lace dress before looking up at her aunt.

"Nervous?" Aunt Ruth asked as they headed toward the judge's chambers.

"Yes, a little."

"Well, don't be. You look like an angel from heaven. Trace will be pleased, I'm sure." She smiled. "I just spoke with him. Good Lord, he looks handsome all dressed up in that dark blue suit of his. I almost wish I was marrying him myself."

Jade gripped her small bouquet of miniature ivory roses and baby's breath. "I . . . uh, I hope I'm making the right decision."

"You are, darlin'. Don't worry."

"This isn't what I had in mind," Jade said, stopping. "I tried to find another way, Aunt Ruth. I don't want to ruin Trace's life. But I have to take care of my son."

"I know that. You don't have to explain it to me," Aunt Ruth said, and gave her a quick hug. "Remember, I was there from the beginning. In the delivery room. I've changed that little boy's diapers. I know all that you've been through. With Fuller and Iris, Rick, your pregnancy, everything."

"I don't want you to think badly of me."

Aunt Ruth rubbed her hands up and down Jade's arms. "Let me tell you something, Jade. I feel as though you've been the daughter I never had. You and Lucas are the family I never had. We'll always be family no matter what happens. And not once was I ever, ever embarrassed or ashamed of anything you've done or any decision you've made. I believe in you. I want you to know that."

Jade hugged her aunt. "I know, Aunt Ruth. I can't tell you how much I love hearing you say that. I had just hoped things could have been a little different."

Aunt Ruth gave her a funny look, then smiled. "What did you expect, darlin'? True love and passion, hmm?"

Aunt Ruth gave one of her hearty laughs and hugged Jade one more time.

"I don't know," Jade answered. "Maybe."

"Well, give that handsome man a chance," Aunt Ruth said. "He might surprise you."

Maybe her aunt was right, Jade thought as they turned the last corner. The hollow sound of her ivory high-heeled shoes clicking against the worn linoleum echoed in her ears. They walked through the last oak door of the old City Hall and into the judge's chambers.

Trace stood when they walked inside.

Releasing a deep sigh of relief, Jade shut the door.

She'd never seen him look more powerful or more handsome. His almost black hair contrasted sharply with his stark white shirt, showing off his tanned skin. It was the first time she'd seen him dressed in a suit and tie. He exuded self-confidence and control.

She didn't want to fall in love with him. She didn't even want to feel any attraction toward him.

She swore under her breath, knowing she'd fought those feelings from the moment she met him at Sue's B&B.

But when she met his dark blue gaze, she felt that familiar stirring deep inside her. It was becoming commonplace for her to feel that ache of desire whenever he was around. She fought for a steady breath, damning her body for betraying her.

Standing beside Judge Desmond was Sue, dressed in a royal-blue dress as her maid of honor. Sam Dorian, the county clerk, had been called in to stand with Trace.

For a moment Jade thought about Lucas. She felt his absence, but knew it was best for him to be at his friend Jimmy's house for the next couple of days.

Her eyes burned with misty tears when she thought about her seven-year-old son and his bright smile. Her heart swelled with love and affection. She couldn't remember a second in her life when she hadn't loved her son. He filled her waking hours with laughter and smiles, with little-boy fears and constant questions. They shared a special bond and a special closeness that could never be matched.

This was for Lucas.

She looked up and caught the inquisitive look on Trace's face.

She felt drawn to him, like a moth to the proverbial flame. She walked toward him, pulled closer and closer to the tempting heat. Aunt Ruth said something but Jade kept on walking. She'd grown so much in the last eight years, and she hoped that she was finally making the right decision.

Lord, but she was beautiful.

Trace had never thought otherwise. He'd only tried not to let it affect him.

He told himself it wasn't how sexy she looked, though the thought of making love to Jade was enough to make his head spin. Instead, it was the way she handled herself in a difficult situation. It was her innocence, and her gallant struggle to protect and take care of Lucas that tugged him emotionally closer to her.

Her dark hair was piled on top of her head and pinned back with a couple of roses. Her skin was silky looking and had a pale glimmer to it, making her appear young and vulnerable.

There was no doubt in his mind that a vulnerable Jade was even more dangerous than a sexy Jade.

He could see she was nervous with each deep breath she took as her breasts strained underneath the ivory silk and lace of her dress.

Still, despite her vulnerability, her naïveté, he couldn't help but wonder if she was wearing satin and lace underneath her dress.

He reached out to take her hand, and a heady warmth spread through him at the contact of her soft, small hand in his.

She didn't say a word, but stared straight ahead.

"I want you near me," he murmured, pulling her

closer to him. Turning to face the judge, he felt a strange sensation go through him as though he and Jade were lovers sharing a secret.

She looked up at him, and he gazed down at her as compassion and heat stirred in him.

"All right," she whispered.

"We're going to be husband and wife," he said, his voice hoarse with emotion. He wanted to say those words to her, to reaffirm what they were about to do, and to give her the chance to back out. "Any regrets?"

She shook her head.

"Don't want to call it off? You can, you know."

She stood fast, leaning ever so lightly against his arm. "No."

"Good."

The air in the judge's chambers thickened and grew hotter with each passing second.

They didn't stand before an altar, or in front of a man of the cloth. There were no stained-glass windows, no organ music to accompany them. There weren't hundreds of guests to witness what was about to happen. Only a select few.

And though his father couldn't have been there, Trace decided he'd call his father in the next day or so and explain why he was helping Jade. He hoped his father would understand.

Sunlight filtered through the shades, throwing heavenly light into the judge's chambers. It seemed to solemnize what they were doing.

Judge Desmond nodded to them and began the ceremony.

The words were formal, precise. Trace heard them. He and Jade repeated their vows.

"The ring, please," Judge Desmond said.

Trace reached inside his jacket, withdrew a wide gold band, and placed it on Jade's finger. He heard her soft gasp, knowing the simple ring surprised her. In what felt like seconds Judge Desmond pronounced them husband and wife.

"You may kiss the bride," the judge said.

The words echoed in Trace's ears as he turned to gaze at his wife.

Jade's eyes were wide, like huge green pools of desire. In that brief moment everything caught and held. Gazes, words, and thoughts were suspended like an electrical current in the warm air. He heard Aunt Ruth and his cousin Sue whispering their glee and happiness. Out of the corner of his eye, he could see Sue snapping pictures.

"I want to kiss you," he murmured to Jade, smiling softly.

He knew he caught her off guard by the rosy glow that spread quickly across her pale cheeks.

"Okay, why not?" she whispered after a slight hesitation. "A simple kiss would be all right."

He grinned and pressed his mouth against her ear. "A simple kiss, hell."

Before she could answer, he pulled her into his embrace, pressing their bodies together in an intimate way, shutting out everything and everyone in the room.

He could feel the slight curve of her waist, the fullness of her breasts pushing against his chest.

He couldn't touch her without wanting her, and he wanted her more than he'd wanted any woman before. He couldn't deny his feelings any longer, and the look in her eyes told him the same.

All pretenses slipped away as he cupped her cheek, turning her face to meet his.

She had soft eyes, innocent and green. She looked so right, and he knew what was about to pass between them would change them forever no matter how much they both tried to deny their feelings.

The kiss was light and tender. The fire was ignited for all to see and for him to feel. He knew this was one fire he couldn't possibly put out. One he didn't want to put out.

He could hear her ragged breathing, feel the wild beating of her heart against his chest.

He wanted more of her. He wanted all of her.

Her lips opened in invitation, and he pressed harder against her mouth, tasting and savoring the sweetness that was Jade. He couldn't remember ever before feeling the sweet desire that rushed through him.

He drank in the taste of her, savoring the weight of her slight body against his. Passion grew and swept throughout his body.

He heard a slight moan rise from her throat, and he released her.

Gazing down at her, he could see the blush spread quickly across her cheeks as an instant and unwelcome tension filled the air.

The anxious look on her face told him she was guarding her emotions and that she'd been surprised by his passionate kiss. She was desperate to disappear back inside her shell.

But what had he expected?

"Congratulations," Judge Desmond said. "You make a fine-looking couple."

The judge's words made him guilty for some reason. But why? He'd done what she'd asked of him.

So why did he feel like he was taking advantage of her?

EIGHT

"I want to show you something."

Jade looked up from her ring to Trace. She could hardly believe he'd actually gone through with the wedding. She'd been married for less than four hours, and he was still by her side. Almost three hours longer than the first time she'd married.

She gazed out the window of his truck, not seeing much as she tried to focus her mind. "Where are we going?" she asked. Her life had changed so fast, she mused. In less than three and a half hours after being toasted as the bride and groom, they'd changed their clothes and were driving out of town.

Trace clicked off the air-conditioning, rolled down the window, and let the early-evening pine-scented breeze inside the truck.

"It's somewhere special," he said, swinging off Taylor Creek Road toward the edge of the thick woodlands. "I thought about kidnapping you in one of the hot-air balloons they have on the South Shore, or on one of those two paddle wheelers, the *Tahoe Queen* or *Dixie II*. But then I thought better of it."

She caught a glimpse of his smile. "Is the surprise better?"

"Yeah." He swung the truck off the road to a secluded area under a huge stand of towering Englemann spruces and lodgepole pines. He leaned close to her, their shoulders touching as he glanced out the windshield.

She held her breath. His nearness was intoxicating.

He cut the engine. "I did find something better that I'd thought you'd enjoy."

"I thought you were doing this for Aunt Ruth."

He gave her a puzzled look. "Aunt Ruth? Why?"

She shrugged. "I thought that maybe you were getting tired of listening to all her hints about getting away."

"Well, hell," he said, and grinned. "I have to admit your aunt is one persuasive lady, but I honestly thought you'd be—"

"Interested?"

"Maybe I hoped you'd be interested," he said, opening the door.

He circled the truck to let her out.

"I'm glad you took her hint," she said. "I'm getting more curious by the second."

He grabbed her hand. "Come on."

Faint light still filtered through the tall trees,

guiding them along a trail that was overgrown with wild peach blossoms and desert lilies.

Winding their way through the thick under-growth and pine needles, they reached the ridgeline above the lake. Trees crowded the edge of the trail and the arching branches made a soft canopy above them. The trail then branched off and twisted in another direction, down the embankment toward the lake, until it disappeared into the wilderness.

Birds darted everywhere, squirrels jumped from one branch to another, skittering to safety as they settled in for the night.

"This is Mother Nature at her best," Trace said. "A testimonial to the existence of God."

"I couldn't agree more."

"Look at the sky."

"I know where we are," she said. "Lucas and I found ourselves not far from here one time. How did you find it?"

"Stan Dryer showed me after I signed the rental agreement earlier this week. We're not far from his place. In fact, the cabin is just around that last bend of trees."

"The view up here is superb."

"It's like the jewel of the Sierras, isn't it?"

She leaned against the wide trunk of a spruce and gazed out at the lake.

"It's awesome."

He took her hand. "Come on down here a little ways."

The subtle scent of his aftershave mingled with

the mountain air, searing her soul. "Where are we going?"

"Just come on."

He led her through a small pasture to the top of a hill.

At the crest of the knoll stood the Dryer cabin, with its high sloping roof. A veranda encircled the entire house, the front of which faced west. Lush green grass dotted with Indian paintbrush and larkspur surrounded the cabin. They followed the flagstone path to the porch. From there, she could easily see the rugged mountains and their boulders surrounding the pristine lake in the distance. It was an unforgiving place, but beautiful and seductive.

"What a view," she said.

"Here. I want you to sit down and watch the sunset," he said, pulling up a couple of lounge chairs.

"It's beautiful."

"I know. This is where I've been coming. It helps to clear my mind."

"Oh," she said, feeling a contented sigh of relief go through her. "I . . . uh, I thought you were with Tamara Wilkes."

He chuckled. "Just watch the sunset."

On the far side of the lake reflections of the mountains rippled across the blue water. The unexpected silence surrounded them as the sun danced off the water's edge and disappeared.

For what seemed like an hour they sat without talking as the coolness of the night surrounded them.

"Would you like to see inside?" he asked.

She tried to think of something intelligent to say, but simply nodded instead. She didn't understand why she was at a loss for words. The fact that they were alone seemed to be her only explanation. Truly alone for the first time.

He opened the door. "As you can see, the place is still furnished. In the meantime I've moved some of my belongings in."

"Very cozy," she said, her gaze traveling over the sofa with its multipatterned pillows and thick, plush cushions. A pine coffee table sat in front of the sofa, and a stone fireplace reached the high wooden beams of the ceiling. Braided throw rugs covered the wood floor, and curtains shaded the large picture window in front.

"There are a couple of bedrooms with one bathroom down the hall," Trace said, nodding toward the opposite end of the house. "And a library upstairs in the loft."

She glanced over her shoulder. "Stan's wife, Effie, was the town librarian right up until her death. She loved books."

"Coffee?"

"Sure," she said, and followed him into the kitchen.

Bleached-pine cabinets, beige-colored walls, and the same country theme continued into the warm-looking kitchen. Blue-and-white checked cushions covered the seats of the wide-back wooden chairs, and a blue-and-white-checked tablecloth covered the oval wooden table.

A short while later they were seated at the table sipping their drinks.

"Are you going to live here?" she asked.

"Not until you settle your custody battle. I don't trust your ex."

"Neither do I," she said, looking around the room. "But it's so peaceful here. How can you stay away?"

"It's hard." After a second he added, "I think it's fair that you know that on the tenth I'm leaving for Portland."

A shot of panic went through her. She cradled the hot mug in her hands, willing the warmth into her suddenly-chilled bones. "That's three days before I meet with the mediator."

"I'll be back to hear what the mediator has recommended."

"You said you were 'leaving' for Portland. Is this a permanent move?"

He pushed his mug to the side and leaned his elbows on the table. "It's a job interview." He shrugged. "That's why I agreed to rent for the time being."

Jade took an uneasy breath. "That's what Sue was talking about. The Portland Fire Department."

He nodded and looked at something over her head. "I have to see if . . ."

She watched his expression change, and he suddenly seemed far away. His voice had sounded tired and emotionless too. She touched his hand, jerking his attention back to her.

Despite her fears, the look he gave her filled her with a raw emotion that she needed to hold in check.

He leaned into his chair and ran his fingers through his hair. His demeanor seemed to change instantly.

"But before I go," he said, "I need a haircut. Know anywhere else besides the Cutting Edge that will do a decent job?"

"Oh, I don't know," she said. "Maybe. Think there are any scissors in this house?" She stood and walked to the kitchen drawers. Opening one, then another, she found a pair. Brandishing them, she turned and smiled. "Afraid of Hank Sewell?"

"Yeah, I'm afraid of Hank. He should get someone else to work for him who can hold a pair of scissors without shaking. Last time, which was the first and only time I went to him, he nearly cut off my ear."

"Afraid of me? My hand is steady."

"No." His voice held a challenge, and his gaze was calm but piercing.

She couldn't help but grin. "Good. Now drag that chair closer to the sink so I can wet your hair."

"I have some shampoo," he said. His eyes were gleaming. "In the bathroom. Do you mind?"

Before she could tell him to go get the shampoo, he'd left and returned with a man's shaving kit in his hand.

He moved the chair flush to the sink and sat with his back against the counter. "Do you know what you're doing?" he asked with a significant lifting of his brows. He pulled the bottle of shampoo out of the canvas bag and handed it to her.

"Of course. I cut Lucas's hair and my own all the time. It saves money."

She found a towel in a nearby drawer and draped it across his broad shoulders and arms. She tucked the end over the collar of his chambray shirt, her fingers brushing his warm skin as she worked. A hot tingle rippled up her arm.

Straightening the towel over his shoulders, she accidentally rubbed her bare arm against his beard-stubbled cheek.

"You could use a shave too," she whispered in a voice that sounded too hoarse to be her own. A muscle clenched in his jaw.

"I just shaved this morning."

"Your beard must grow fast."

"Are you offering?"

She hesitated. Their conversation was venturing into unknown territory. "I've never shaved a man before. I definitely don't know what I'm doing there. So I should stick to haircuts. And so should you. It's safer that way."

"I haven't been safe from you since day one."

She could feel his gaze on her and hear the seriousness in his voice, but thought it better to ignore both.

"Here, tilt your head a little farther back," she said as she tried to elude further contact with his body by shifting sideways. She turned on the faucet and tested the water temperature.

He leaned back to allow her to soak his hair.

"How's that?" he asked, his voice deep and utterly sexy.

Still avoiding his stare, she tangled her fingers in his silken black hair, running the water through it. "Perfect," she whispered. "Though your hair is clean. I shouldn't be washing it."

"Sure you should. It'll feel good."

Control, she told herself. She could control her thoughts, her passions. Concentrate.

Her gaze finally connected with his.

He made her feel like a woman just by being near him. Delicate and loving. He made her ache with something she couldn't describe, something she'd never felt before. No other man had ever done that.

Control, she whispered silently again and again. It was her mantra. She never lost control of her emotions.

Until now.

Trace's gaze moved over Jade's face, her small chin, her rosy mouth. He swallowed as he watched her every move.

She kept her own gaze fixed on his hair, as if looking at him would break her concentration.

The sweet scent of cinnamon floated around him and he inhaled deeply, allowing her to sear his heart forever.

He closed his eyes and let his senses take command. Over the heavy pounding of his heart, he could barely make out the sound of her uncapping the shampoo and setting the bottle on the counter.

She rubbed the creamy substance into his hair with small circular motions. Hot tingles shot across his scalp. The heat traveled swiftly down his neck and back. It was as though he was being caressed by fire.

He moaned softly as the aching tension grew in the lower portion of his body.

She ran her fingers through his hair a few times, brushing his whole scalp, working back from the hairline as she went.

"I think I used too much shampoo," she said, quickly rinsing off her hands.

"I don't care," he murmured. "Just don't stop."

"You like?"

"You kidding?"

Laughing softly, she took one section of hair at a time and gently pulled. She rubbed the strands between her fingers as she washed.

"What are you doing?" he asked, still keeping his eyes shut.

"A little of this and a little of that," she whispered, her voice sounding raspy but sweet.

Delicately, she ran her palms across either side of his head, caressing the tender area behind his ears.

"Here, lean back a little," she said. "I have to rinse your hair."

Moving to a better position, he caught her hand before she turned on the water.

Their gazes locked.

"I don't think you know what you're doing," he said.

"Sure I do," she protested. "I told you that I cut Lucas's hair all the time."

"That's not what I meant."

"I have to rinse your hair," she said, ignoring him.

After thoroughly soaking his hair and then drying him off, she combed out the tangles.

Then, with each snip of the scissors, a lock of hair tumbled to the floor.

"You're good," he said quietly as he watched her in a hand mirror.

She moved around the front of the chair, unintentionally bumping into his knees. She smiled. "I know."

Automatically, he parted his thighs, allowing her to step in between his legs to get a better angle.

She stood directly in front of him, her legs rubbing against his as she worked. He could feel her fingers weave through his hair, lifting and separating the strands with each cut.

Staring straight ahead, he could see where she'd splashed water on her off-white blouse, soaking her clear through.

In spots, the thin material stuck to her skin, outlining the curves of her bra and her breasts. He could see her pulse at the hollow of her neck beating wildly. With each breath she took, he saw the soft swell of her breasts between the parted folds of her silky blouse. And with every slight movement of her body and her arms, gentle waves of her perfume surrounded him.

It was at that exact moment he felt the thin thread of his control snapping.

He swallowed. The heat she stirred in him was hotter than any blazing inferno he'd faced. And it was growing hotter by the second.

Making love to Jade right there on the floor of Stan Dryer's kitchen flashed through his mind. Gritting his teeth, he knew he'd just have to sweat it out.

But then he realized it was probably too late. Too late to turn away and ignore what had been happening between them from the beginning. Perhaps he'd known all along that he was going to have a relationship with Jade, maybe even the first time he'd gazed into her emerald eyes.

It didn't seem to matter anymore that he'd sworn not to get near her, not to touch her in a way that would make her forever his.

"You have a lot of hair," she said, her voice whispery soft. "There's one section here that's giving me a hard time."

She moved slightly, her breasts brushing closer to his face.

He smothered a groan. Her nearness provoked more sensations and reactions inside of him. More than he could ever imagine.

She stopped mid-cut and looked at him. "What'd you say? Did I pull a Hank Sewell"—she giggled—"and cut your ear?"

He swallowed, the humor lighting her face and

eyes making him want her even more. Worse, he needed her. The combination was deadly. "Ah, it's nothing."

"I swear I thought you said something," she said, moving even closer between his legs.

"No, I didn't."

"Okay." She leaned near to his face to make one last cut. "I thought you were starting to think I was bothering you."

"Oh, but you do bother me," he said, reaching up and tucking a long lock of hair behind her ear. "But not the way you think."

She put the scissors on the counter and stared at him.

He closed his legs tight around her, trapping her. The contact sent a gut-wrenching sensation through the muscles of his thighs and straight to his groin.

"I'm finished," she said.

"I'm not. And neither are you."

Her soft gasp made his body come fully aroused.

He put the mirror on the counter and dropped the wet towel in the sink. He brushed the back of his hand against her cheek and her eyes slid shut. "Look at me, Jade," he whispered.

"I can't."

"Why do you fight so hard against what you really want?" he asked, staring at her mouth.

Her soft, kissable mouth.

He shuddered, willing himself to remain seated. He watched her face as she struggled for what little measure of control she had left. She opened her eyes.

"We can't do what I see in your expression, Trace."

He cupped her face, pulling her to him.

Her skin was smooth, and he automatically touched his lips to her temple, brushing ever so lightly. "You always tell yourself to do the right thing?"

"Yes. For as long as I can remember."

"Well, it's time you stop. It's time for you to be bad for once."

"Trace."

There was a pleading sound to her voice, but he ignored it. He ignored their agreement and ignored the warnings in his mind. "It's okay," he said. "We're married."

She was close. So close he could feel her breath on his face. He remembered the softness of her lips, how her mouth felt. Slow and delicious. Deep and erotic.

"It's not okay," she whispered. Her mouth brushed against his.

"But it *is* okay," he insisted, letting the husky sound of her voice ripple over him and into his heart.

He tasted the sweetness of her lips and her tongue as it swept along the inside of his mouth.

Her lips left his to touch underneath his ear. He shuddered at the contact. "Take what you want. Take me."

"Yes," she murmured.

"I belong to you now," he said, closing his eyes.

"We're husband and wife, no matter what anyone says. It's okay."

"Oh, I . . ." She gasped, pressing her body fully against his chest and kissing him more deeply.

His arms encircled her waist, and he pulled her onto his lap. "You want me, Jade, as much as I want you."

"Yes, I want you. I want to be bad. Oh, so bad."

Jade felt like she was spinning, tumbling in space. Trace was sin and salvation all wrapped together. And she was going to follow him wherever he led. And if making love to Trace was bad . . .

Then she was bad.

With both hands, she grasped his head, drawing him to her. The stubble of his beard was rough under her caressing fingertips, but it felt marvelous, delicious, prickling her heated skin.

She pressed her breasts against his chest. He was solid and incredibly masculine.

His hands traveled up over her hips, freeing her blouse from her jeans.

She ran her fingers along the inside of his shirt collar. The warmth of his body shot straight through her hands and the rest of her body. She could feel the pounding of his heart as she unbuttoned and removed his shirt.

As she caressed his shoulders and the upper portion of his back, she felt the burn scars. She tried not to think of the pain he must have gone through, and pressed kisses across his neck and shoulders.

He didn't seem to mind her exploration of his injuries, and responded to her kisses with a soft groan of pleasure.

"Sweetheart," he murmured, "that feels . . . unbelievable."

A shudder passed through her as he slowly undid the buttons of her blouse. Warm air hit her bare skin as her shirt slipped to the floor in one easy motion.

A passionate fluttering arose at the back of her throat. She opened her eyes, and he made no attempt to hide the fact that he was watching her and that he wanted her.

His hand, warm and smooth, slid underneath the waistband of her jeans. She stood, and a rush of heat surged through her as he undid the brass button and zipper, then slid her jeans down over her hips and legs to the floor.

She rose on her tiptoes, giving and offering herself to him as she easily stepped out of her jeans and her satin panties. She felt proud of her body. For once, she didn't feel she was lacking.

"Let me see your beauty," he said. "All of it."

He crushed her to him, reclaiming her lips. His tongue explored the recesses of her mouth, and she gave herself freely to the passion of his kiss.

"Let yourself go," he murmured, running his mouth along the side of her neck. His hands, big and warm, traced up her back with a featherlight caress.

He released the clasp of her bra, dropping the lacy lingerie to the growing pile of clothing on the floor.

She arched her back as he cupped both breasts, drawing a soft cry from the back of her throat.

"You feel so right," he said.

"You make me feel right," she answered.

He stroked one breast, fingering her nipple ever so gently until she hardened under his touch.

But things started going a little too fast, and before she realized what had happened, he, too, was naked, his jeans and shorts having fallen to the floor as well.

His body was hard, his skin warm and smooth as she trailed her hands down his neck and his back, drawing him close to her.

He made her ache with hunger, and she longed to discover the rest of him.

She moved against his hands as he explored her back, waist, breasts, teasing her into a frenzy. His lips were moist and warm as he kissed her breasts, her nipples, then lower down her belly. He pulled her back onto his lap, kissing her with weeks' worth of pent-up passion. Scalding heat seared her wherever their flesh met.

"Wrap your legs around me," he whispered, his voice hoarse with need.

Trembling, she encircled his waist with her legs.

She could feel the gentle touch of his hand sliding down her bare back to her buttocks. She could feel her heart beating erratically.

He kissed her again. Greedily, hungrily.

His fingers trailed across her belly, branding her skin with his touch until he found the soft downiness between her legs. Running his finger deliciously up and down between her thighs, he traced a path over her skin before slipping one finger inside her, exciting her, making her ready for him.

Fully aroused, she drew herself closer to him. "Trace," she whispered.

"Are you ready, sweetheart?" he asked, nuzzling her throat. "Because I am."

She moaned. "Yes, yes."

"Hand me my bag," he said, his voice dropping low with need.

She reached behind his head and grabbed his shaving kit. His breath fanned the nape of her neck.

"What are you looking for?" she asked.

"Protection, sweetheart."

She felt her face burn. "I . . . um, I didn't think of that," she said, thankful that one of them had a tiny ounce of sense left.

Within seconds he found what he needed and slipped the condom into place. He lifted her, then grasped her hips in his large hands and guided her to him, their gazes locked together.

His eyes widened at their first intimate touch.

She stiffened instinctively. He slowed, then gently eased her onto him. Warmth spread throughout her. Still holding her hips, he carefully helped her match his own rhythm.

A low moan of pleasure escaped his throat.

Jade watched the change in his eyes, surprised to see the strength and caring in those blue depths.

"Jade?"

The sound of her name sent shivers up her spine.

"Yes?" she whispered, pressing her fingers against his lips.

He suckled her fingers, and heat pounded through her. She knew the feel of his touch would be burned in her memory forever.

He kissed her breasts, her throat, then captured her lips as he thrust strong and deep inside her. He kissed her thoroughly as she moved with him in a graceful, easy dance. She tangled her fingers in his hair.

"Don't stop, Trace," she said, letting a soft cry of desire tear from her.

"Not yet, sweetheart."

She clamped her teeth on her bottom lip and shut her eyes against the desire sweeping through her. She arched her back as he pulled her closer to him.

"Jade," he said. "Now, sweetheart."

"Yes, now," she said, and gave herself into her needs and his.

Tiny ripples of spasms erupted within her as the world spun out of control. The hot-white pleasure exploded all around her, leaving her breathless and panting for air.

She slumped against his chest, resting her head in the cradle of his neck.

For a few seconds she listened to his heavy breathing and the pounding of her heart. She knew her desire had merely been whetted, not quenched. That part was simple. She also knew that her feelings were deep and complicated.

And dangerous.

So, while he merely filled her with a moment of physical desire, she was allowing him to tear apart her soul.

If this was bad, then she'd be damned to hell forever.

NINE

"Hold the marshmallow a little closer, honey," Jade said, bending next to Lucas in front of the stone fireplace of the cabin.

"Here," Trace said. He took the long metal prong from Lucas's hand and swept it over the low-burning flames. He handed the prong back to Lucas.

"Like this?" the boy asked, imitating Trace.

Trace took his hand and gently pulled it back from the flames. "Not too close. And you have to keep turning it so the marshmallow doesn't get burned on one side or catch on fire."

Lucas giggled and settled himself on the floor in between Jade and Trace. With his free hand, he draped his arm over Trace's right knee, leaning into him for support. He yawned loudly and crossed his legs at the ankles. "I've never been camping before. 'Cept Aunt Ruth took me to Lake Tahoe for a Cub Scout meeting."

"This isn't exactly camping, honey," Jade said, watching the exchange between her son and her husband.

Husband.

The word was so strange, and frightening. But nice at the same time.

She glanced over the top of Lucas's head and found Trace watching her. Ever since she and Trace had made love the night before, she'd fought the urge to tell Lucas the truth about her marriage. But in the end she realized that making love to Trace had been a sudden burst of desire and had nothing to do with what she would tell her son.

"But this is the second best thing to camping, huh, Lucas?" Trace asked, looking at the boy.

"Yeah," Lucas said.

The little family-style activity they were sharing right now was enough to set her mind into rapid confusion. She bit the inside of her cheek. Her concerns were growing. With each passing day, Lucas was showing more affection toward Trace.

It worried her, knowing that within a few days it could all be over—once the judge and mediator made their decision about her life and her son's.

Then Trace would be gone.

Lucas took the prong and twirled it between his fingers as he closely inspected the marshmallow. "How's that?"

Trace narrowed his eyes. "Hmm, let's see." He checked the marshmallow. "Nice golden brown.

Looks good to me, unless you like 'em crispy and black."

Lucas wrinkled his nose. "Yuck, no."

"This is your last one, Lucas," Jade said, rising from the floor. "Then it's time for bed."

Lucas groaned, but his frown changed when he popped the treat into his mouth. "One more, please, Mommy?"

Jade shook her head.

"Trace promised he'd play another video game with me."

"It's time," Jade said. "Now scoot."

"Really?" Lucas begged, obviously stalling for time.

Jade nodded. "Really."

Lucas stood and held his hand out to Trace. He grinned and said in a fake deep voice, "I want to thank you for inviting me to sleep over at your house."

Trace took one look at the small sticky hand extended in front of his face.

"Lucas," Jade said. "Go wash your hands—"

"Anytime, pal," Trace said, shaking the boy's hand before Jade could stop him.

She couldn't help the smile that spread across her face.

Trace smiled back at her before glancing at Lucas. "Now get out of here, wise guy. And go to bed."

Giggling, Lucas skipped down the hall.

Jade shook her head. "I don't know what I'm going to do with you guys."

Several minutes later, after tucking Lucas in bed, she found Trace stretched out on the couch cushions in front of the fireplace. It looked as though he were in a trance.

She was suddenly filled with a sensual awareness of him and had to fight the urge to stare at him and admire him.

She didn't want to focus on his lean body dressed in shorts and T-shirt. She didn't want to see his muscled arms and chest and powerful-looking legs. Nor did she want to smell the soap he used or the aftershave that was distinctly his.

He shifted his weight, as though he sensed she was standing there. He didn't get up, but simply watched her as she approached.

"That didn't take long," he said, his voice soft as smoke.

She watched him run his hands through his newly trimmed hair, remembering his tender and titillating touch. "Lucas is pretty well behaved when it's time for bed. Especially when he knows I mean business."

Trace laughed, a low and smooth sound. She liked listening to it.

"He'll be asleep in two minutes," she said, sitting down next to him. "He's had so much fun hiking all those secret trails you showed him today. He sleeps like a rock."

"What about when I woke him up that first night at Aunt Ruth's house? I scared the you-know-what out of him with my nightmare."

She turned to look at him. "You scared the you-know-what out of him the first day at Sue's, period. That night he was just concerned about you."

"He's a sweet kid."

"I've never seen him happier," she said as she snuggled into the deep cushions of the couch. "Except that one Christmas when he got his bike. Now, that was one happy kid."

"He's a good boy, Jade. A real pleasure to be around."

"Thank you for bringing us up here before you leave for Portland," she said. "It's so peaceful."

"This is a great place to fall asleep and dream. It's like you're in heaven, or at least what I'd imagine heaven to be like."

"Have any dreams about me?" she asked.

The pupils in his eyes dilated with a look of desire. "Oh, yes, ma'am, I have," he said. "At least they're close enough to remind me of you."

The sound of his voice said more than his words.

"Oh, yeah?" she asked. "What about?"

"I have this fantasy, a recurring fantasy." He took a strand of her hair and rubbed it between his fingers. "About this woman with long hair the color of midnight."

He brought her hair to his lips, kissing softly.

"And what does this woman do?"

A sly sexy smile curved his lips. "She draws me into the woods and . . ."

"And what?" she asked, knowing he was teasing her.

"She undresses me and then makes love to me."

"I don't believe you."

He shook his head. "The truth, I swear. Almost every night. The same dream."

He wrapped her hair around his hand and tugged her to him until their lips almost touched.

"Believe me," he said, the sound of his voice seeping deep into her senses like a soothing balm.

He put his hands on her shoulders, drawing her to him. She wasn't surprised when his mouth dropped over hers and he kissed her. It was insane not to think that she wanted this to continue.

"Trace," she murmured, "what are we doing?"

"I don't know," he whispered, trailing his lips down her neck to the low V of her shirt.

"This is crazy," she said.

"I know." Grasping her waist, he pulled her onto him as they settled next to each other, lengthwise, across the sofa. "What about your son? Will he wake up?"

"Depends on how much noise you make."

He froze.

She giggled. "I told you he won't wake up, guaranteed. Besides, we'd hear him coming down the hall."

He found her mouth again, kissing her deeply. He tore away. "I hope you're right."

Jade watched the change in his eyes as his hands slid up her back and removed her red shirt in one motion.

He lowered his gaze to her bare breasts and swung her underneath him. "I want to taste you."

"Yes," she murmured as his lips closed over one nipple with a gentle kiss.

He traced a fiery path down her belly, pulling her red shorts off as he went. Looking up at her, he grinned.

She could feel her heart melt.

He bent over her again, claiming her mouth with his.

Knowing that she was just about to break every rule in her book and that she was probably certifiable, she gave him more than her body.

She gave him her soul.

And her trust.

She was worse than any drug.

And ten times as addicting.

Trace watched Jade as he dropped his shirt to the floor. She snuggled closer to him. The provocative angle of her hips cradled against his arousal was more than he could bear. Her eyes were shut in anticipation as she invited him to her with an uplift of her hips,

"You are like heaven," he murmured, running his hands over her back, pressing her to him.

Heart to heart.

Soul to soul.

"Am I?" Her voice was husky and filled with passion.

His hands explored the lines of her back and her waist while he traced a path down her neck with his lips.

With trembling fingers, she unfastened his shorts, moving the zipper down with ease as though she'd done it a thousand times before. Her caresses became bolder. She uttered an earthy groan, and ran her hands underneath his briefs.

She dropped his clothing to the floor on top of the terry robe she'd carried from the bathroom. She opened a small packet and slipped the condom on him.

"Damage control?" he asked.

"I come prepared."

"Smart lady," he said, his voice raw with desire.

Gently she grasped him and guided him to her, arching her back as she did so.

Tucking her curves neatly into his own contours, he felt as if he was ready to lose his mind. "You are incredible."

He entered her, inhaling sharply as he did.

A bright flare of desire sprang into her eyes and she rose to meet him in a moment of uncontrolled passion.

She couldn't disguise her body's fire. And he was glad. She was perfect.

He moaned his surrender at her heat, her fierce tightness, at her closing in around him in one bold stroke. He took her mouth with a savage intensity, forcing her lips open with his thrusting tongue. His emotions were like a runaway roller coaster, careening off track.

She put her arms around his neck, drawing him to her. "Trace," she whispered. Her breath was hot against his ear.

Stunned by the ferocity of his need for her, he rocked back and forth, murmuring her name. He'd never felt this good. Never imagined that he would.

"Trace, you take my breath away."

Her voice caressed him as his pleasure shattered and exploded into a million fiery lights.

A few seconds later they collapsed together, sinking into the cushions of the couch.

"I want you," he said in between harsh gasps. "I want you to be mine. I lov—ah . . ."

He stammered and stopped speaking on a staggered breath. He couldn't say those words, though they came straight from the feelings deep in his heart.

She sighed and shifted, slipping on his terry robe.

For several minutes he didn't say anything and neither did she.

In the silence he wondered what kind of woman Jade was. She was so delicate but strong, and fought for what she believed in. He'd known that the moment he met her. The thought of the burdens she carried made him determined to hold her forever.

There was no doubt she'd wanted to make love with him that night. He hadn't seen the first hint when she'd brought his robe. But the condom . . . now, that was something different altogether.

He'd told himself to avoid commitments. So what had he gotten himself into? If it wasn't possible for them to build a strong relationship for the long term, then it was stupid of them to waste their time pursuing anything beyond brief moments of intimacy.

He'd made a deal with her. He was going to stick around until the job was finished. At the very least, he was deeply concerned for Lucas's welfare.

Marriage had to mean much more than that, though. His father had been right about Valerie when he'd made the comment after she and Trace got engaged that she wouldn't support his career. And Val walked out on him. He couldn't risk Jade doing the same thing knowing that a firefighting job could take him away from her at any time.

Perhaps he could commute and stay in Faith on his time off, he reasoned, if the Portland job offer sounded good. That way he could still see Jade, Lucas, and Aunt Ruth, even his nosy cousin Sue.

But no, he decided, nothing could work between them. The sooner he let those thoughts be known, the sooner he could stop his own emotions—and maybe hers—from growing out of control.

He gently touched the top of Jade's head as he watched the embers glowing in the fireplace. Her hair was soft as silk, her skin like satin to the touch. And the scent of her perfume pervaded the room.

"I've always liked watching a fire," she said, breaking the silence.

"I thought you were asleep."

"I drifted off." She sighed. "I was more tired than I realized."

She rolled onto her back and gazed at him. The terry robe parted. He angled himself into a more comfortable position on his side and pulled the robe shut, closing her off physically and emotionally.

"Do you find fire as mesmerizing as I do?" she asked. "Is that why you became a fireman?"

He wanted to laugh but didn't. She wouldn't understand the absurdity of her question. Nor would she understand what they'd just shared in the last hour could never happen again.

"Yeah," he said, after struggling for an answer. "I find fire fascinating but frightening at the same time."

What a jerk he was. He'd made a mistake in bringing her and Lucas to the cabin. He knew that now. He'd made a mistake in allowing himself to be overcome by sexual desire when he knew making love to Jade was wrong.

She grasped his hand. "I can't imagine what it's like to do the job you do."

He didn't reply.

"I'd like to hear about it."

He knew he had to let go of the past just as he had to let go of her. Talking about it would help. "I can still remember that hot summer afternoon, one year ago, like it was yesterday."

She sat up to look at him. She didn't say a word, but her eyes told him she wanted to hear more.

"The weather had been unusually warm, just like

it's been around here lately. It's something I'll never forget. The wind had blown close to the ground. There was smoke first, then the fire, with embers filling the sky. The smoke had blocked out the sun, but the flames lit everything." He spoke slowly, remembering every detail.

"Does it scare you?" she asked.

"Every time." He took a deep breath. "And there was this eerie orange-gray cast to the buildings, the fire trucks, everything. Once close to fire, I could feel the intense heat, smell the smoke. It was hard to see because of the smoke clouding my goggles. I remember feeling the sweep of water being dropped from the helicopters. And the loud pops and snaps of burning wood and the groan of the house as it . . ."

"As it what?"

"Collapsed around me."

"Oh, my God."

He glanced at her. He hadn't realized that he'd been staring at the fireplace the entire time and that he'd purposely avoided telling her the entire truth. She didn't have to know all the agonizing details. It wasn't important.

He rose from the couch and pulled on his briefs and shorts. Walking to the hearth, he rested his hand on the carved oak mantel.

"What's wrong?" she asked. "You don't have to talk about this anymore."

The sound of her voice tore at him, making him turn around to face her. Her eyes were dark, more than the usual emerald color. Like evergreen.

He didn't want any other man near her or her son. He wanted to take care of them both himself. But he had to say something now before their false relationship went any further.

Suddenly he was angry that he cared about her and Lucas when he was used to caring for only himself. He was angry that he had to fight to ignore all the implications of those feelings. A sharp pain ripped through his gut. He knew he had refused to face the truth. Refused to acknowledge his mistakes and refused to acknowledge one important fact.

He was falling in love with her.

His emotions were strong and enduring, growing by the minute, and it wasn't something either of them could ignore.

But he could stop it.

And right now.

"Ah, hell, Jade, it's not just about the fire," he said, his voice raw.

"Then what?"

"I don't think I can do this."

She sat upright, and he could see panic slipping across her expression.

"Do what? What are you talking about?" she asked.

"What do you want from me?"

"I don't know wh—"

"One minute we're here with your son, roasting marshmallows, then we're talking, and the next minute you're in my arms and everything goes crazy. All with your kid in the next room."

"He didn't wake up," she protested.

"That's not it. Every time we're together it gets crazy."

He paced the room and turned to face her. "I know I'm handling this badly, but we have to talk."

"About what?"

"This." He spread his arms, gesturing. "Us."

"About how it shouldn't happen again?" she asked, her voice shaking.

"It's useless, and I think you know why. I could be leaving. You won't need me any longer after the court makes its decision."

"Trace, please," she said, clenching her fingers. "I don't want to talk about this."

"But I do. We have to settle this before I leave for Portland."

She grasped the edges of the robe together as though she couldn't bear for him to see any of her bare skin.

"We both know things got out of hand," he said. "We both know for everyone concerned, including Lucas, this can never happen again."

"That doesn't explain why it happened."

"No, it doesn't."

She shrugged, feigning indifference, though he knew better. She was protecting herself, and it wounded him knowing that what he was doing was cruel.

"You know, it was just sex," she blurted out. "A certain chemistry that sparked between us."

He didn't want to hurt her, but he didn't know of

any other way. It was for the best. "Yeah," he growled. "Animal attraction."

She stood and walked toward the hallway. "Okay, then, I'll just forget any of this ever happened, just chalk it up to both of us going a little crazy."

"Yeah," he said. "A little crazy."

She didn't say another word, but turned and disappeared into the darkened hallway.

He watched her walk away, feeling strange and lost.

His heart felt equally as dark.

Trace's palms itched.

His body stiffened. His eyes flashed open. He tried to adjust to the darkness in the living room.

A spasm of alarm blazed up his spine and tiny beads of sweat popped out on his forehead. His heart raced and his blood pounded through his veins.

He knew he couldn't be experiencing another one of his nightmares because what he was feeling was too real, too intense. He could never miss the stench of smoke. It was impossible. But not impossible for there to be a fire.

He shot upright from the couch.

Forcing himself to think, he turned on the table lamp.

Thin curls of smoke slithered, like snakes, along the floorboards. Crawling forward from the kitchen, the haze slowly swirled upward, growing thicker by the second.

He took in a quick sharp breath, the smoke sting-ing his nose and his throat. He choked and then coughed as he tried to catch his breath. Jumping from the couch, he fell a few steps forward. His eyes stung and watered.

Get up. Run. A paralyzing fear gripped him. He couldn't move. It felt as though he'd leaped into a vat of concrete.

Somehow, he managed to push himself up. Tak-ing a couple of steps, he found himself standing by the fireplace, but his legs couldn't move another inch.

His mind screamed. *Run!*

His reactions left him reeling and bewildered. He was going to die if he didn't do something quick. He didn't know where the fire had originated, except it was coming from the side of the house near the kitchen.

Jade.

Lucas.

Run. Get them out. Move your legs.

Thunderstruck, he could no longer ignore his past or his mistakes.

"Jade!" he shouted, stumbling to the first bed-room door.

Testing the handle for heat and finding none, he flung the door open.

Jade was sound asleep, one leg and arm hanging over the side of the bed. It was clear she hadn't heard a thing.

He rushed to her side, grabbed her by the shoulders, and yanked her clear to the floor. "Jade, wake up."

"Trace!"

Her face was pale and drawn.

He grabbed her elbow and jerked her out of the bedroom and into the hall.

"Get out!" he shouted. "Get out now!"

"Is there a fire?"

He heard the panic in her voice. Or was it his own?

"Somewhere on the other side of the cabin."

"Lucas!" she screamed.

"I'll get him. You get out. Now!"

A loud pop followed by crackling wood sounded from the rear of the house. Smoke billowed down the hall, rising like clouds toward the ceiling.

"Go out toward the living room and dial nine-one-one," he ordered.

"Get my son," she shrieked above the hissing noise of breaking glass and burning furniture. "Please."

He whirled around and ran down the dark hallway.

Jade and Lucas sat on the grass in front of the cabin, waiting for Trace to finish talking with the fire chief.

The back portion of the cabin smoldered in the early-morning air.

Trace, assisted by the firefighters, had managed

to extinguish the flames. They'd fought the blaze from the middle of the night until dawn.

Through the early-morning shadows, smoke curled like ugly black ribbons among the embers and charred wood along the side of the cabin.

Nothing in the kitchen had been saved.

Trace sat beside them in the dewy grass. "Are you two all right?"

Jade nodded. "Lucas was saying that his eyes stung. But I think he's okay."

"What about you?"

At first she didn't say a word. She just stared at him. "Don't worry about me, Trace. I'm fine."

She knew by the tone of her voice that he could detect her lie. He knew exactly what she really meant. Whatever had transpired between them, both good and bad, was over. But wasn't that what he'd wanted?

"I want you to go with the paramedics anyway. Just to make sure. Let them take you and Lucas to the hospital."

"If you think that's best."

The sharp stench of smoke clung to him and his clothes. "I do." His voice was cold and distant.

She stood and took Lucas's hand. "What did they say?"

He glanced at her, his eyes bloodshot and tired. "Preliminary inspection points toward arson. An arson inspector will be here within the next few hours."

"Arson?" she repeated. "But how? Who would . . ."

He sighed and rubbed his hands across his face. "I don't know."

"When?"

He shook his head and swore loudly as he looked around. "Damn, how can I explain this to Stan? I've been here less than a week and look at the destruction."

His voice sounded weary, but she knew it went deeper than that.

"It wasn't your fault."

He stared hard at her, and from the expression on his face she knew he was blaming himself.

"You said so yourself," she said. "The preliminary—"

"Means nothing to me right now," he practically shouted at her.

"I better get Lucas to the hospital."

He stood. "That's a good idea. And as soon as the arson unit arrives, I'm leaving for Portland."

"I know," she said.

She watched him take the steps of the cabin two at a time and disappear inside.

TEN

By the time Jade had finished her morning deliveries, she was dead tired.

She cut the engine of the van and got out. Her heart ached. Her whole body ached. It had been nearly three days since the fire and she hadn't heard a word from Trace.

It was also her big day with the mediator and the judge. Trace had said he'd be back by the time her meeting was scheduled.

She couldn't help but remember that last day with him, before the fire had broken out at the cabin. She had wanted to tell him how she felt, but she hadn't. She'd refused to ask him to stay with her and love her for real. She'd asked so much of him already. Her pride just couldn't take any more rejection.

She remembered his closed expression when he'd left. His eyes had been cool, ice blue with indifference. A wall had been thrown up between them. They were strangers again, each fighting for his own survival.

"You are not going to believe it," Aunt Ruth said when Jade walked in the back door of the bakery.

Jade propped the empty trays against the wall and walked toward the huge table where her aunt was mixing a fresh batch of dough.

Aunt Ruth wiped her hands on a towel and picked up a piece of paper. "I just got a phone call from the sheriff's office."

"What about?" Jade asked. She slid into a chair and picked up a sticky cinnamon roll from its baking pan.

"The arson unit investigating the fire at the Dryer cabin has been in contact with the Doral County Sheriff's Department."

"What did they find out?"

Aunt Ruth pulled up a chair and sat down. She waved the piece of paper. "Briefly, according to the experts, they can tell how and where the fire originated. Then there were some witnesses who stated they saw a man buying containers of kerosene and other combustible materials in quantity while staying at Lake Tahoe."

Jade felt her heart race. "Trace had said it was possible arson was the cause behind the fire, which only meant someone was after me or him." A trickle of sweat rolled down her back.

"The sheriff has arrested the suspect, who, by the way, is someone we all know."

"Oh, my God," Jade said. "I feel sick."

Aunt Ruth nodded. "Rick."

"But why?"

Aunt Ruth crumbled up the paper and tossed it across the table. "Lord only knows why." She reached across the table and grasped Jade's hand. "You're shaking, darlin'."

"I know. I'm terrified."

"Well, the good guys have got him now."

"But why would he want to harm his own son? It doesn't make sense. He wanted to get custody of Lucas. He wanted the money."

Aunt Ruth shook her head. "Maybe he knew he was going to lose custody anyway. I never thought he'd win."

"But we don't know that. I'm supposed to meet with the mediator and judge this afternoon."

"Rick's not going to win now, for sure," Aunt Ruth said, pushing herself up from the table. "That scoundrel is finally where he belongs. Behind bars."

"But how do they know he was the one who set the fire?"

"According to the deputy I spoke with, there were two other witnesses who said that a man who fits Rick's description was seen earlier that day around the Dryer cabin."

"But we were at the cabin most of the day," Jade said. She dropped her head into her hands. "We didn't hear or see anyone. Except . . ." She looked up at her aunt. "Except those couple of hours when Trace took us hiking."

Aunt Ruth shrugged and went back to her baking. "So, darlin', your problems are solved."

"Oh, I don't know about that. What happens when he gets out of jail?"

"He won't for a long time."

"You don't know that."

Aunt Ruth leaned both palms on the table and stared at Jade. "He hasn't made bail, and I doubt he will. He'll go to trial and be put away for a long while."

"You sound like a lawyer who doesn't know what she's talking about."

"You, Lucas, and Trace will continue to have a home here with me," Aunt Ruth said, ignoring her last comment. "I'm so happy. Aren't you?"

Jade stood and looked at the new addition, her mind and heart filled with the memories of Trace and what they'd shared. "Yes, I'm happy."

The lie stung.

"It's funny," Aunt Ruth said, rolling out the dough, "how everything turns out perfectly."

"Yeah, perfect."

The words sounded as hollow as she felt.

Trace wedged his truck in the last available spot in the courthouse parking lot between an old station wagon and a new Suburban. He got out and shut the door. He was going to miss this quaint little town and its easy pace and friendly people. Even the likes of Tamara Wilkes and Kit Moreland.

He took the steps to the courthouse two at a time. Worse yet, he was going to miss Jade.

The musty old courthouse was busy as he walked through the double doors and into the crowded corridor.

"Trace, over here," Sue shouted.

Turning around, he saw his cousin waving at him. Sitting next to her, on a bench lining one wall, were Aunt Ruth and Lucas.

He took a deep breath and walked toward them.

He could see the panicked look on his cousin's face, the worry in Aunt Ruth's as she wrung her hands, and Lucas's inattention as he stared at the wood-plank floor.

"Where have you been?" Sue demanded. Her eyebrows were knitted into a frown. "You promised you'd be here."

"I'm here."

"Yeah, but it's late."

"Now, Sue darlin', " Aunt Ruth said, wrapping her arm around Sue's shoulder. "He's here and that's what counts."

Trace looked down at Lucas, who was clinging to Aunt Ruth's other arm. "How's it going, pal?" He ruffled the boy's white-blond hair.

Lucas shrugged.

Trace stooped down and looked straight at him. "Aren't you going to say hi?"

Lucas looked away. "Hi."

Trace stood and glanced at Aunt Ruth.

"He thinks you're leaving," she said.

"But I—"

"For good, Trace. The boy thinks you're leaving us all for good."

Dread filled him. "Aunt Ruth, this is complicated enough as it is. I—"

He stopped when the door to the judge's chambers opened.

Jade stepped out with her attorney, Morris Peterson.

Trace's gaze met Jade's. The tense lines on her face relaxed for a second, then she looked away. His chest felt as if it would burst. She was no woman to fall in love with. He'd offered her everything he could. His comfort, his strength, his name. But never his heart.

He walked up to her. A cold knot formed in his stomach. "I'm sorry I couldn't get here sooner like I promised."

Silence loomed between them like a heavy mist.

"It's all right," she said.

The words came out barely louder than a whisper and tight with pain. He could tell she was upset and nervous by the way she avoided his gaze.

"The judge . . . uh, he . . ." She turned and looked at Morris.

"Glad to see you're here," Morris said. He shook Trace's hand. "I believe the judge and mediator would like to have a few words with you."

"All right." He looked at Jade. "Do you want to go in with me?"

"It isn't necessary," she said, her voice faltering.

She glanced down the hall as though she was preoccupied. "The judge wants to clarify a few things with you. His decision has already been made."

The anxious look on her face told him she knew that his decision had been made too.

The only problem was telling her what she already knew.

Tears welled up in Jade's eyes.

"Don't cry, Mommy," Lucas said. He slouched down on the couch next to her.

"It's okay, sweetheart," Jade said, hugging her son. She wiped her face. Her last encounter with Rick, as she'd left the courthouse earlier that day, had been enough to set her off.

He'd been vicious and nasty, yelling all the right words as the sheriff's deputies ushered him inside the prisoner van headed for Lake Tahoe for his next hearing.

But she'd stood up for herself and hadn't backed down from his threats. She knew she wasn't a wimp anymore.

A short while later she saw Trace leave the courthouse. He had a short conversation with Morris, then he'd told her he'd see her later. She knew why he wanted to see her.

She'd won her custody battle. She kept telling herself that was the only thing that mattered. And strangely enough, Trace had been appointed as temporary trustee for Lucas's trust fund. She didn't know if he had accepted the responsibility.

She gave Lucas another hug and kissed the top of his head. "Isn't it time for bed, young man?"

He sighed. "Yeah, I guess so. Aunt Ruth said she'd let me have an extra cinnamon roll if I brush my teeth real good."

"All right," Jade said, patting his bottom as he slid off the couch. "I think she's in the kitchen. I'll come up in a little bit to say good night after Aunt Ruth puts you to bed."

He hitched up his pajama bottoms. " 'Kay."

Jade stared out the screen door. The wind chimes sang a soft song with the evening breeze. It was getting cooler. She rose to shut the door.

"Are you going to lock me out before I have a chance to talk to you?"

She froze.

Trace stood on the front porch.

"I didn't hear you come up the walkway," she said. She tried not to stare at him, the casual way he leaned against the porch support, or the way he had his large hands shoved into the pockets of his jeans. It only made it harder knowing what he was going to tell her.

He stood there for another second, watching the wind chimes jingle against one another. "I didn't bring a jacket," he said.

She touched her forehead in mock stupidity. "Oh, sorry. Come on inside. You surprised me, you know."

He walked into the living room and sat on the couch, stretching his long, muscular legs in front of him.

She didn't want to look at him, or think how wonderful she felt when he held her in his arms. But she did anyway. She couldn't stop herself.

His dark hair glistened like polished ebony under the glare of the table lamps. He lifted a framed photograph from the end table and stared at it.

"He's a good-looking kid, Jade."

"He looks a lot like his father."

Trace put the picture down. "But he's beautiful inside, like his mother. I'm going to miss him."

"He'll miss you, too, Trace." She willed herself not to say anything that would make him believe she wanted him more than anything in the world.

She loved him. She knew that now.

She tried to swallow the knot that had formed at the back of her throat.

"Is Lucas here?" he asked.

She ran her fingers through her hair. "Aunt Ruth is putting him to bed."

"I'd like to say good-bye."

"You accepted the Portland job?"

He nodded. "I had to take the job. I was born to do that job. It's in my genes. My father knew it and I know it too. I'll be able to get back to doing what I do best."

"I'm glad for you, Trace." She hesitated, wishing she could prolong his stay, but she knew she couldn't. "Did you take the job for your father?"

At first, she thought she saw a look of apprehension slide across his face. Then he seemed to pull his emotions into line. Strong and serious.

"At first, yes, I thought I had to do this for my father," he said. "I didn't think I could get back on the line again until the fire at the cabin. It made me realize how important the job is and that I could do it. Then I wanted to do the job for myself."

"We need people like you," she said, stopping herself from saying we need heroes like you.

"Before I leave Faith, I'd like to square things with Lucas. He wasn't too happy the last time I saw him."

"I wish you wouldn't."

Trace sat forward and frowned, looking at her intently. "How come?" he asked in a controlled voice.

She turned away, unable to face him. He swung her around, and shock registered up and down her body. He'd been so quiet, she hadn't heard him come up behind her. He kept his hand on her elbow, and she felt her legs sway underneath her.

"How come?" he asked again, dropping his hold.

"I just think it'd be easier on him to have you sort of disappear."

"Or easier for you?"

She tried to stop her gasp of surprise. "Look, I admit the one huge mistake I made in asking you to marry me was the effect it would have on Lucas."

"I can see that now too."

"I had no choice," she said. "I had to make the

decision of asking you to marry me or risk losing him. Now I have to ease Lucas's fear of losing another person. I didn't have any other choice. I know we promised to take care of the little details, like the annulment, when this mess was over."

"Which we are going to do, right?"

She bit down on the pain marching its way through her heart like an invading army. "Yes. That's what we said. I'm a big girl. I've taken some hard knocks along the way. I can handle this."

"Can you?"

"I have to. But my son doesn't. He grew too close to you, Trace. I don't know how he's going to take your leaving. But I'm going to do whatever it takes to protect him."

She sat on the couch.

"I don't agree with you, but he's your son and I'll respect that. I just want you to know I, too, don't have any other choice. I have my own life to lead. We both knew that from the beginning. I've agreed to oversee Lucas's trust fund until another trustee can be appointed. It's the least I can do. You don't have to worry about his interests. And you won't have to hurry the process. I'll be there for him as long as it takes."

She looked up at him. He seemed farther away than just a few feet. "I know," she said. "And I appreciate your efforts, really. I just have to deal with the consequences and hope that Lucas will be okay."

"I'm sorry, Jade. We all had our problems we

needed to work out. I hope Lucas won't hate me because I have to go. He's one great kid."

He headed for the kitchen. "I just have a few things of mine I left packed in the kitchen. I'll pick them up on my way out after I say good-bye to Aunt Ruth."

She rose to her feet, her heart aching with pain. "All right."

Something flashed in his eyes, but he quickly masked it before she could determine what it could mean. She wanted one last kiss good-bye, no matter how bittersweet it would be, but knew he didn't share her wish.

"I'm glad I met you," he said.

"Me too. Thank you for helping me save my son."

"Take care, Jade O'Donnell."

He swung through the kitchen door before she could whisper back, "Take care, Trace Banyon."

Jade had faced her nemesis, her own weaknesses, and won. She'd finally taken charge of her life. So, she couldn't exactly say she regretted anything she'd done in the past twenty-eight years.

Except one thing.

Every day that passed, she still thought about Trace and tried not to think that only three weeks had gone by. It felt like three years.

"Here's your cup of coffee," Sue said, handing Jade her usual mug.

Jade sat down at the table. "I hurried with all my morning deliveries to get here," she told Sue, who was busy preparing breakfast for the last of her summer guests. "I can't believe he actually came."

"Me, neither," Sue said. "It took a lot of convincing. You owe me."

Jade smiled. "Dinner and gambling at Tahoe. Name the time and we'll go. Guaranteed."

"Don't think I won't take you up on your offer," Sue said. "Here, sit. I have to serve up some of Aunt Ruth's cinnamon rolls and get the decaf. He's very picky, you know."

Jade kicked her feet up on a nearby chair. "You and your relatives."

"Good morning," a rich, deep voice said from behind her.

Sue stopped pouring the decaf into a mug and glanced over her shoulder. "Ah, there you are."

Twisting around in her chair, Jade stared into the bluest pair of eyes she'd ever seen. Well, almost.

The man was older, in his sixties. He was handsome, tall, and broad-shouldered. He held out his hand. "You must be my daughter-in-law."

"Uncle Tyrone," Sue said, putting the coffeepot down. "This is Jade."

Jade shot Sue a nervous glance and shook his hand. "I don't know what to say except I'd like to thank you for coming to see me."

Tyrone pulled up a chair and sat down. "I was more curious than anything." His expression seemed frozen. He didn't smile, but simply looked straight at her until she felt a nervous flutter in the pit of her stomach.

"I still appreciate your efforts."

"I see no reason to hedge around the reason why I flew hundreds of miles to see you."

"I understand," she said, bracing herself for his obvious questions.

"I don't understand this marriage between you and my son. Not one bit."

Jade flinched at the tone of his voice.

"Uncle Ty," Sue said, circling the table and putting her arm around his shoulders. "Jade needs to ask you some questions about Trace, and since I knew you were going to Portland to see him, I thought this would be a good chance for you to try to understand what their marriage was all about."

"Suze, Jade's a big girl," he said, his gaze never leaving Jade. "She married my son, and I'd like to know why. Let her talk."

Sue frowned. "All right. I think I'll go check on my guests." She gave her uncle a hug. "Now be nice. Or else."

An unwelcome shiver ran through Jade. From the little she'd gathered from Sue, she knew where Trace got his strength and his convictions. Tyrone Banyon was tough and direct.

"You're not pregnant, are you?" Tyrone asked.

Jade folded her hands on the table, willing herself to be strong. "No."

"For someone who had to get married in a hurry, I just expected that to be the case."

"It's not."

"I want to know why my son married you."

She hesitated for a moment, scrambling for an answer. "Before I answer that, let me ask you this."

He nodded and leaned back in his chair. He had a powerful presence. Just like his son.

"Have you seen Trace?"

"Yes."

"In Portland?"

He nodded.

"Then you know why he married me. He had to have told you the reason."

"Yes, but I wanted to hear your side."

"I needed a husband to keep from losing my son," she said, feeling as though she'd shoved cotton into her mouth. She walked to the sink and filled a glass with water. "It wasn't any more mysterious than that. At least in the beginning."

She took a huge swallow of the water, relieving her dry mouth. It had been so simple in the beginning, before she fell in love with Trace.

"I understand you won your custody battle," he said.

"That's right."

"Trace is the trustee of your son's trust fund." He leveled his cool blue stare at her. "That's a heavy responsibility."

"That's right," she said. "I told Trace how much I appreciated his efforts."

"So what do you want to know? What can I tell you?"

"I'll be getting an annulment before long. But before that happens, I need to know why Trace left."

"I think you have to understand one thing here, young lady, and that is, I come from the old school. I'm old-fashioned. I believe that commitments, however made, should be kept. I believe my son is strong in spirit and heart. He's very generous, and bargain or no bargain between you two, I thought this marriage was the craziest thing I'd ever heard."

"I know. And it was until I fell in love with him. That's why I need to know why he left."

He continued to stare at her. "Marriage has to mean more than a bargain. I know. I was deeply in love with Trace's mother until the day she died. Perhaps he couldn't take the chance of you leaving."

"But that's different. Your wife didn't leave you by choice."

He nodded. "The idea is the same. I believe the accident is part of why he's resisted admitting that he loves you."

Jade sucked in a deep breath. He couldn't possibly know how Trace felt about her. "Did he tell you that he loved me?"

"Not in so many words."

"So how would you know?"

"Because I've never seen him so distraught in his entire life."

Jade found herself speechless.

"I knew the young woman and her son who died in the accident," Tyrone went on.

.

"What woman? I thought only Trace was seriously injured in that accident. . . ."

"A young woman and her son died," Tyrone said.

"He didn't tell me that."

"That doesn't surprise me. I knew the woman. Not well. She was an artist well-known in the community. Her career was beginning to take off. Her son was about your son's age. Their deaths made the papers. Front page. It was tragic. Young woman, raising her son on her own, defeats odds by becoming a success in her field. Strange. The resemblance is uncanny."

"What resemblance?" she asked. She couldn't help but wonder how much pain Trace held inside himself.

"Have you ever experienced déjà vu?"

"Sure. From time to time."

"I have too. Such as right now when I look at you."

"Why? I don't understand."

"Because the woman and her son who lost their lives, in that fire, looked just like you and Lucas."

A cold silence swept the room.

"And," Tyrone said, "my son believes he let them die."

ELEVEN

A man, Jade decided as she looked in the bathroom mirror, was the last thing she needed in her life right then. Why she had ever agreed to come to Sue's surprise birthday party when she knew there would be eligible bachelors was beyond any reasonable explanation, other than she needed to move forward with her life.

It was too late to back out of the party. She was committed whether she liked it or not. She'd spent over an hour getting ready, with the hope that putting on some pretty clothes and doing her hair up would at least lift her spirits.

Still, she felt just as hesitant about going as when Sue had first suggested it over a week before.

She checked her reflection again, picked up her half-empty glass of champagne, and left the bathroom, heading down the hallway to where Sue's party was in full swing.

It had been over a month since she'd last seen Trace. Almost two weeks since her bizarre conversation with his father, Tyrone. Thoughts of their conversation constantly filled her mind. No matter how she decided to live her life, she knew she had to get Trace out of her mind. And out of her heart.

"That dress you're wearing tonight is lovely, darlin'," Aunt Ruth said.

Jade stopped at her aunt's side and gazed out at the game room where Sue was busy chatting with some of her guests.

"Almost sexy," Aunt Ruth added. She gave Jade a slight smile.

Jade ran her hand down the tight-fitting black knit and swayed a little.

"You've been drinking," Aunt Ruth stated. She took the glass from Jade's hand and placed it on a nearby table. "You don't drink."

Jade grinned mischievously. "I am tonight."

Aunt Ruth raised expressive eyebrows. "Is that why you're wearing that slinky outfit with those black strappy things on your feet?"

Jade stuck her foot out at an angle. "You mean my evening sandals? I got these rhinestone beauties in a boutique in Lake Tahoe."

She stopped speaking and leaned against the wall for support.

Maybe she had been drinking too much. But she needed something to calm her nerves.

"The dress, too, I suppose?" Aunt Ruth asked.

"Of course." She pushed herself away from the

wall. "Besides, my outfit isn't meant to be sexy. I wanted to wear something that'd lift my mood."

"Uh-huh. I heard what's-his-name, Sue's friend, comment on it."

"Anthony De Landa," Jade said.

"So when are you going to introduce me to Mr. Eight-Hundred-Dollar-Suit-and-Salon-Styled-Hair? He sure has been hanging all over you this evening."

"I know," Jade said, letting out a tired sigh. "He's making me uncomfortable."

"And what does he do to dress that way?"

She glanced at the man, noticing for the first time Anthony's expensive suit and Italian leather shoes. All she ever seemed able to think about was a broad-shouldered man who normally wore a T-shirt and faded denim. A man with hair the color of midnight and incredible blue eyes that scorched her soul with fire every time he looked at her. "He's an Internet consultant from Sacramento," she told her aunt.

Aunt Ruth grunted. "Oh, please. Like I know what an Internet consultant is."

"With the computer world exploding, Sue says his future is pretty good," she said, nodding toward Anthony, who'd just looked up and waved at her.

"Is he part of your future?" Aunt Ruth asked.

"Aunt Ruth, I just met him. I really don't need a man right now. Besides, the annulment hasn't even happened yet."

"You're still stalling."

Jade glanced at her aunt and shrugged. "I haven't had the time to see Morris yet."

"Right."

"Really."

"You miss Trace, don't you?"

Jade tried to mask her pain but knew it was a waste of time. She wanted to crawl into a dark hole and never surface again. She couldn't hide anything from her aunt. And she couldn't hide from herself any longer. "You'd know I was lying if I said I don't think about him."

"Yes, I would."

Jade's eyes widened, and she stifled a groan. "You wanted to meet Mr. Eight-Hundred-Dollar-Suit?" she whispered in a hoarse voice. "Here he comes. Now be polite."

"Of course, darlin'. I'm always polite."

"Then how come my palms are sweating?"

Anthony De Landa strolled up, holding a glass of white wine in his hand. He slipped his arm around Jade's shoulders and eased her closer to him. "And who is this lovely vision?" he asked, winking at Aunt Ruth.

Jade stiffened and shot him a sideways glance. "Anthony, this is my aunt Ruth O'Donnell."

Aunt Ruth smiled at him, but Jade knew the sincerity wasn't there.

"For the love of Pete," Aunt Ruth said. "That's the worst— Ouch. Jade, what are you doing? Don't pinch me."

"What were you saying?" Anthony asked. He grinned at Aunt Ruth, then took a sip of his wine.

Aunt Ruth stepped out of Jade's reach and turned her blazing gaze onto Anthony. "I was saying that was the worst come-on line I've heard in all my fifty years," she said.

Anthony chuckled and turned his attention to Jade. "I heard your aunt was a feisty old gal. Guess the rumors were correct."

"Anthony," Jade said, "I think Sue is calling—"

"If you want to keep that arm of yours, mister, then you better get it off my wife," Trace said with a hard edge to his voice.

Jade froze and held her breath.

She turned and saw Trace standing in the front doorway, his broad shoulders filling the wide expanse. She stared at him in astonishment, wondering if drinking too much champagne could cause hallucinations.

A T-shirt, worn black denim, and scuffed cowboy boots looked wonderful, indeed, she decided.

"Did you forget something?" she asked Trace, feeling as though her heart was going to shatter into a thousand pieces as she waited.

He looked at her. "Only my wife."

Trace wanted to strangle the man who'd dared touch Jade. She belonged to him, and he was determined to make her, and everyone else, understand that.

But his anger softened the moment he saw her face. It had been over four weeks since he'd left for Portland, over four weeks since he'd seen Jade.

It seemed like a lifetime.

He'd wanted his life back, with no more nightmares, no more guilt, and no more visions of Jade. But going to Portland wasn't the answer.

He hoped returning to Faith was.

"You're married?" Anthony exclaimed, stepping back. "I don't get it."

Trace glared at the man. "I'm her husband," he said, his voice growing louder. He grabbed Jade's hand, happy to see that she still wore his ring. He held up her hand. "Now do you understand?"

Several party goers turned their heads to watch, obviously curious about the growing ruckus.

Anthony raised his hands in self-defense. "Hey, man, I didn't know. I swear."

"Forget it," Trace said, concentrating on Jade.

Anthony mumbled under his breath and quickly excused himself.

Trace's gaze swept over Jade, taking in the black dress that hugged her breasts and slim hips, the sparkly high-heeled black sandals on her feet. He glanced at Aunt Ruth and gave her a quick kiss on the cheek.

"Good to see you, Aunt Ruth. I missed you."

She pinched his cheek. "Same here, kid."

"Speaking of kids," Trace said, refocusing his gaze on Jade. "Where's Lucas?"

"He's upstairs sleeping in Sue's room," Aunt Ruth said.

"Then I'll catch him later."

"I think I better check on Sue's birthday cake," Aunt Ruth said, excusing herself.

"What are you doing here?" Jade asked.

"I came here for you."

"For me?"

"Yeah, you," he said, smiling. "Who else? You are still my wife."

She glanced around the room. "And everyone knows it."

"They'd better. Especially strange preppy types."

Jade started to laugh. "Anthony isn't a prep—"

"I don't care about him," Trace said, taking her by the elbow. "I want to show you something."

He led her outside to where his truck was parked. "Get in."

"Is this another one of your kidnappings?"

"Looks like it, doesn't it?"

When he pulled into the graveled drive of the Dryer cabin fifteen minutes later, Jade slid out of the truck as he shut off the engine.

He was intensely aware of the sights and sounds surrounding him as he watched Jade make her way across the yard. He could hear the soft rush of wind whispering through the pine needles, the distant sound of mountain bluebirds settling down for the night. The rich scent of wild peach blossoms and desert lilies from the nearby meadow filled his senses, making him wonder why he hadn't noticed them before.

And then he knew.

It was all because of her.

"I can't believe it," she said as she carefully trotted up the flagstone walk to the front porch.

She turned to face Trace, who was a few steps behind her.

"I can't believe it," she said again. "It's gorgeous."

Joy bubbled in her laughter and shone in her eyes.

He'd hoped tonight there would be no shadows across her heart.

"It looks perfect," she said. "Like there wasn't a fire at all. What happened?"

He opened the front door and nodded for her to enter. "Just a lot of hard work, some insurance money, and savings from my old job. You won't recognize the back side of the house where the fire originated, though I haven't gotten around to getting appliances or painting it."

"What old job? Portland?"

He shook his head. "No, when I was with the force in Seattle. I had a settlement from the accident and savings accumulated by the time I left."

"I thought you were strapped for money."

"In a way I was. I didn't want to touch that money in case of an emergency. And this was an emergency."

"I thought you were only renting this place. What happened?"

"I bought it. It was the only way not to put Stan on the spot. Buying the place was another way to force me to look at my life too."

She shook her head and walked toward the fireplace. She placed her hand on the mantel. "I'm surprised." She turned around. "What about the job in Portland?"

"I quit."

"Why?"

"Why? You ask why?"

He walked toward her and rested his hands on her shoulders. He took in a deep breath, remembering the sweet scent of her. His heart raced.

"My soul wasn't in it," he explained. "But that's not the only reason. I finally realized that running away wasn't the solution to my problems. It wasn't going to take away my guilt. I knew life had to go on."

"I guess we all have to learn that at one time or another," she said.

"I know," he said, looking deep into her green eyes. "And then I thought becoming a firefighter again was the answer. Then I thought going to Portland was."

"Was it?"

He shook his head. "There was still something missing."

"What?"

"You."

She didn't say a word.

"I couldn't understand my feelings of resentment when you wouldn't tell Lucas about our marriage."

"That's funny. Why?"

"At first, I didn't know. I thought, why should I care? But then I realized that in my heart I didn't want this to be a marriage in name only. I wanted to be a true husband and a true stepfather. Your refusal to tell Lucas told me that you didn't consider it a real marriage. And that hurt."

"So why did you marry me? Was it to ease your guilt over the woman and her son who died in that fire?"

He groaned and dropped his hands from her shoulders. "I should have told you everything about the accident. I wasn't completely honest. I'm sorry."

She walked away and sat on the couch.

When she gazed up at him with those green eyes of hers, he could feel his breath catch. He couldn't move. His heart was hammering so loudly in his ears, he could hardly hear or think straight.

"At first it was my guilt," he said. "When I finally acknowledged to myself that I was with you for the wrong reasons, that I was trying to make up for the past, for what had happened to the woman and her child, I realized I loved you despite the coincidence and not because of it. Of course, it took being away from you to learn that and that I shouldn't doubt my feelings."

"What if you leave again when I need you?" she

asked. "I've been through that before. I can't do it again."

Forcing his feet to move, Trace came and sat beside her. He wanted to pull her into his arms so badly, it hurt. He could hear the concern in her voice, and he felt as if he was falling in love with her all over again.

"I know," he said. "I can understand your anger and your frustration."

"It's real, Trace."

He grasped her hand, feeling the familiar heat connect them. "Jade, we both have to learn to trust a little more. I realize I can't keep you at arm's length just because I might lose you. I came back for you. Doesn't that show you something?"

"Yes, it does."

His heart pounded. "I need you by my side. I need Lucas too."

She hesitated as though struggling to find the right words. A sigh that sounded like relief broke from her lips. "Do you?"

He put his arms around her shoulders and pulled her to him, burying his face in the warmth of her neck. "Say it, Jade."

He lifted his head to look at her. She was breathtaking.

"You want to hear that I was searching for a hero and I found him?" she asked.

He was just a man, a simple man with needs. But she was more than he'd ever hoped or dreamed for.

"Do you want to hear that I didn't realize it right

away either?" she went on. "That my only concern was for Lucas? I needed a father for my son."

"You also need a husband."

"I need you."

She brushed her mouth across his, sending his blood pressure soaring. She touched the tip of her tongue, silky and wet, to his lips.

Then his mouth was on hers, hard and persistent. He caught her lower lip between his teeth and sucked gently. With both hands, he gripped the back of her head, undoing the barrettes that held her black hair. Her wild mane of hair fell around her shoulders.

"Say it," he breathed. "I want to hear you say that you love me as much as I love you."

She did love him, Jade thought. It was crazy, madness.

And she wasn't going to fight it.

She knew by his greedy kisses that he loved her. Only a man possessed kissed the way he was kissing her right then. Deep and hungry, thrusting his tongue into the recesses of her mouth, and no longer playful.

She knew she was his woman, and he was her man.

She felt her shoes slip to the floor.

Not knowing how her dress followed suit, leaving her in her black French-lace panties and bra and silk hose, Jade slipped her hands under the T-shirt he wore, bringing it up over his head. The brass buttons of his jeans had just as mysteriously parted beneath her fingers. His pants fell over the edge of the couch, followed by the rest of his clothing.

"How do you know that I love you?" she asked.

"I knew you had to love me by the way you made love to me before, and the way you're making love to me right now."

His words settled on her dizzied senses, making her feel totally alive. No longer were confused thoughts haunting her. No longer did she have doubts about what she had to do.

His lips slowly descended to meet hers with sweet tenderness. She succumbed to his kiss, feeling as if every inch of her body was bursting into flames.

She wanted to pull away from his mouth long enough to tell him how much she wanted to see the bedroom, but realized it was too late.

His hands were on her, searching, coaxing, and loving her. She found herself suddenly naked. The ache, the need for him was overwhelming. Incredible heat seeped through every limb, weakening her beyond belief.

"Yes, I love you, Trace," she said, pulling away for a brief moment. "I know it's right with you."

He cupped her breasts, and instinctively, her body arched toward him as his lips brushed her nipples. She shifted restlessly, capturing his hand and dragging it lower down her body.

He didn't need any further coaxing as one, and then two fingers found the wet softness of her at the juncture of her thighs.

"You have a nice way of telling me what you want," he said.

She wanted more. She wanted to feel him inside her. "I want your arms around me," she panted. She opened her eyes. She wanted this for the rest of her life. "Trace, look at me. I want more. I want all of you. Heart and soul too," she whispered hoarsely, feeling her control flying away.

He turned her in his arms and held her close and tight. His hard body was atop hers as he thrust deep inside her.

"I want it to last forever," she murmured as they stared into each other's eyes.

"Me, too, sweetheart. Me too."

She rose up to meet him, time and time again until he lifted his hips sharply, sensing that she needed the last final explosion.

She gasped in sweet agony as her body melted against his and the world was filled with him and only him.

He collapsed against her, breathing hard. He ran his hand along the side of her face, gently caressing.

"We have a thing for making love on couches and chairs, don't we?" he asked.

She looked at him as a golden wave of passion and love flowed between them. "I was going to suggest the bedroom, but I figured the timing wasn't so great."

He sat up and gathered her into his arms. He kissed the top of her head, and she could hear him take a deep breath.

"We'll have plenty of time to do it in the bedrooms, sweetheart."

"What?"

He glanced at her with an almost hopeful glint in his blue eyes. "You're already home."

"What are you talking about?"

He pulled her onto his lap, kissing the nape of her neck.

"I don't want an annulment, Jade. I want you for the rest of my life. Please believe me."

She looked at him. "You want to stay married?"

"Yes. My God, you're stubborn, woman." He kissed her fiercely on the lips. "What do you think I'm doing here, what do you think I've been saying?"

"I, uh, I don't—"

"I love you very much. And I love Lucas too."

She couldn't believe her ears. "But what about you being a firefighter? What about your dreams and goals? You have to still want those things."

He straightened. "Oh, yeah. I don't think I could go on making flower boxes for people like Mrs. Jacoby. The construction business really isn't for me."

"You did a beautiful job on the bakery."

"Yeah, but being a firefighter is a family tradition. It's what my father had wanted for himself and for me, but more important, it's what I want. It's about bravery, honesty, integrity."

"And now?"

"I still believe in honesty and integrity. But it's not just about being brave when you're fighting fires. I also believe you must be true to yourself while learning to deal with the death, destruction, and tragedy that's all around you."

"You're an honest and good man, Trace. I knew that right from the beginning."

He placed his fingers across her lips. "I know the accident will always be with me," he said. "I forgot my training in coping with troubling incidents. I've learned from my mistakes."

"We all learn from our mistakes. Me, too."

"But for me, being a firefighter isn't just about the grueling physical side of putting on twenty pounds of gear, dragging a two-hundred-plus-pound hose, hammering through a roof with a sledge-hammer, and crawling through attics. It's more. I need more."

"What about Lake Tahoe? You could be a firefighter in Tahoe, couldn't you? I'm sure they need someone like you. It's not that far. Only a few miles."

He nodded. "It's worth checking."

"Yes, yes, it is, Trace," she said, feeling a strange sense of excitement race through her at the thought of staying in Faith with her family.

Family. What a wonderful-sounding word. She smiled.

"Only if I know I have you and Lucas by my side."

"Forever," she whispered. "We'll be by your side, forever."

"I want to make sure you love me, Jade O'Donnell Banyon. I want to make sure you want to spend the rest of your life with this scarred, sometimes stupid man."

"You're not stupid," she said, brushing her lips across his. "Just stubborn."

"Now, where have I heard that before?"

"Hmm? I wonder."

He kissed her.

"I think I'll love you for the rest of my life," she murmured.

"And I'll love you for the rest of mine."

"Forever?"

"Yes, forever."

THE EDITORS' CORNER

To celebrate our fifteenth anniversary, we have decided to couple this month with a very special theme. For many, the paranormal has always been intriguing, whether it's mystical convergences, the space-time continuum, the existence of aliens, or speculation about the afterlife. We went to our own LOVESWEPT authors and asked them to come up with their most intriguing ideas. And thus the EXTRAORDINARY LOVERS theme month was born. Have fun with this taste of the supernatural, but first check beneath the bed, then snuggle under the covers. And don't let the bedbugs bite . . . they do exist, you know!

Brianne St. John is finding herself **NEVER ALONE**, in Cheryln Biggs's LOVESWEPT #890. It's hard enough when just one ghost is hanging around, but what does a girl do when four insistent ghosts are on her case? Ever since she was a little girl, she's had Athos, Porthos, Aramis, and yes, even D'Artagnan to scare all her boyfriends away. Now that gorgeous entrepreneur Mace Calder has set foot in Leimonte Castle, the four musketeers are in an uproar! Mace has noticed that the lady of the house tends to mutter to herself a great deal, but for now he has other important matters to take care of. As Mace and Brianne draw closer, strange things keep happening, objects are being moved, shadows are darkening doorways—and Mace wonders just when is that wall going to answer Brianne? Cheryln Biggs revisits old haunts and legends in this enchanting romp of a love story!

Journalist Nate Wagner has his hands full when he confronts **WITCHY WOMAN** Tess DeWitt, in LOVESWEPT #891 by Karen Leabo. What strikes Nate about the beautiful woman he's followed into a Back Bay antique shop is that she doesn't look like the notorious Moonbeam Majick, a witch who disappeared fifteen years ago. Tess knew she and everyone around her were in harm's way the minute she came across the cursed cat statue that had very nearly ruined her life. Teamed up with an insatiably curious Nate, Tess must find a way to save her best friend's life, prevent Nate from dying, and keep the cat away from the mysterious stranger who's bent on unleashing the statue's unholy powers. In the end, will a spell cast from loving hearts be enough to save them all from certain death? Karen Leabo delves into the mystical connections our souls offer to those we truly love.

Loveswept veteran Peggy Webb gives us **NIGHT OF THE DRAGON**, LOVESWEPT #892. With only a book and an ancient ring to guide her, Lydia

Star falls back in time and lands at the feet of a fire-breathing dragon. Lydia is saved by one of King Arthur's brave knights, Sir Dragon, and is forced to face the fact that she's not in San Diego anymore. Dragon is bewildered by his mysterious prisoner, but can't help being captivated by her ethereal beauty. Convinced that she is the result of some deviltry, he confides in the king's counsel, Merlyn. Lydia knows her time is running out and longs for the comforts of home, a fact that keeps her trying desperately to escape from the overbearing knight's clutches. Can this warrior be the keeper of her soul? Better yet, will he survive the journey to his heart's true home? Peggy Webb more than answers these questions with this sensual dream of a romance.

Catherine Mulvany treats us to **AQUAMARINE**, LOVESWEPT #893. Teague Harris can't believe his eyes when he sees his supposedly dead fiancée walking around the carnival grounds. He's even more surprised when he realizes that Shea McKenzie might not be his former love . . . but she does look enough like Kirsten Rainey to pose as the missing heiress for Kirsten's dying father. Drawn to Idaho by a postcard found among her dead mother's things, Shea reluctantly agrees to the outrageous masquerade after seeing a picture of a man who could pass for her own father. Then, as Shea discovers a cluster of glowing aquamarine crystals, she begins to experience Kirsten's memories. Can Shea trust Teague, a man who seems more interested in trying to solve the murder of Shea's twin than in moving on with the rest of his life? Catherine Mulvany teaches us that love is the strongest force on earth!

Happy reading!

With warmest wishes,

Susann Brailey   Joy Abella

Susann Brailey   Joy Abella

Senior Editor   Administrative Editor

P.S. Look for these women's fiction titles coming in June! From Nora Roberts comes **GENUINE LIES**, now in hardcover for the first time ever. Hollywood legend Eve Benedict selects Julia Summers to write her biography. Sparks fly and danger looms as three Hollywood players attempt to protect what they value most. Talented author Jane Feather introduces an irresistible new trilogy, beginning with **THE HOSTAGE BRIDE.** Three girls make a pact never to get married, but when Portia is accidentally kidnapped by a gang of outlaws, her hijacker gets more than he bargained for in his defiant and surprisingly attractive captive. And finally, Rebecca Kelley presents her debut, **THE WEDDING CHASE.** Zel Fleetwood is looking for a wealthy husband who can save her family. Instead she attracts the unwanted attentions of the earl of Northcliffe, whose ardent but misguided interest ruins her prospects. That is, until he realizes *he*'s the perfect match for her. And immediately following this page, preview the Bantam women's fiction titles on sale in May!

For current information on Bantam's women's fiction, visit our Web site at the following address:
http://www.bdd.com/romance

Don't miss these extraordinary
novels from Bantam Books!

On sale in May:

*A PLACE TO
CALL HOME*
by Deborah Smith

*THE WITCH AND
THE WARRIOR*
by Karyn Monk

Come home to the best-loved novel
of the year . . .

A Place to Call Home
by Deborah Smith

Twenty years ago, Claire Maloney was the willful, pampered, tomboyish daughter of the town's most respected family, but that didn't stop her from befriending Roan Sullivan, a fierce, motherless boy who lived in a rusted-out trailer amid junked cars. No one in Dunderry, Georgia—least of all Claire's family—could understand the bond between these two mavericks. But Roan and Claire belonged together . . . until the dark afternoon when violence and terror overtook them, and Roan disappeared from Claire's life. Now, two decades later, Claire is adrift, and the Maloneys are still hoping the past can be buried under the rich Southern soil. But Roan Sullivan is about to walk back into their lives. . . . By turns tender and sexy and heartbreaking and exuberant, A Place to Call Home *is an enthralling journey between two hearts—and a deliciously original novel from one of the most imaginative and appealing new voices in Southern fiction.*

"A beautiful, believable love story."
—*Chicago Tribune*

It started the year I performed as a tap-dancing leprechaun at the St. Patrick's Day carnival and Roanie Sullivan threatened to cut my cousin Carlton's throat with a rusty pocketknife. That was also the year the Beatles broke up and the National Guard killed four students at

Kent State, and Josh, who was in Vietnam, wrote home to Brady, who was a senior at Dunderry High, *Don't even think about enlisting. There's nothing patriotic about this shit.*

But I was only five years old; my world was narrow, deep, self-satisfied, well-off, very Southern, securely bound to the land and to a huge family descended almost entirely from Irish immigrants who had settled in the Georgia mountains over one hundred and thirty years ago. As far as I was concerned, life revolved in simple circles with me at the center.

The St. Patrick's Day carnival was nothing like it is now. There were no tents set up to dispense green beer, no artists selling handmade 24-karat-gold shamrock jewelry, no Luck of the Irish 5K Road Race, no imported musicians playing authentic Irish jigs on the town square. Now it's a *festival*, one of the top tourist events in the state.

But when I was five it was just a carnival, held in the old Methodist campground arbor east of town. The Jaycees and the Dunderry Ladies' Association sold barbecue sandwiches, green sugar cookes, and lime punch at folding tables in a corner next to the arbor's wooden stage, the Down Mountain Boys played bluegrass music, and the beginners' tap class from my Aunt Gloria's School of Dance was decked out in leprechaun costumes and forced into a mid-year minirecital.

Mama took snapshots of me in my involuntary servitude. I was not a born dancer. I had no rhythm, I was always out of step, and I disliked mastering anyone's routines but my own. I stood there on the stage, staring resolutely at the camera in my green-checkered bibbed dress with its ruffled skirt and a puffy white blouse, my green socks and black patent-leather tap shoes with green bows, my hair parted in fat red braids tied with green ribbons.

I looked like an unhappy Irish Heidi.

My class, all twenty of us, stomped and shuffled through our last number, accompanied by a tune from some Irish dance record I don't remember, which Aunt Gloria played full blast on her portable stereo connected to the Down Mountain Boys' big amplifiers. I looked down and there he was, standing in the crowd at the lip of the stage, a tall, shabby, ten-year-old boy with greasy black hair. Roan Sullivan. *Roanie.* Even in a small town the levels of society are a steep staircase. My family was at the top. Roan and his daddy weren't just at the bottom; they were in the cellar.

He watched me seriously, as if I weren't making a fool of myself, which I was. I had already accidentally stomped on my cousin Violet's left foot twice, and I'd elbowed my cousin Rebecca in her right arm, so they'd given me a wide berth on either side.

I forgot about my humiliating arms and feet and concentrated on Roanie Sullivan avidly, because it was the first close look I'd gotten at nasty, no-account Big Roan Sullivan's son from Sullivan's Hollow. We didn't associate with Big Roan Sullivan, even though he and Roanie were our closest neighbors on Soap Falls Road. The Hollow might as well have been on the far side of China, not two miles from our farm.

"That godforsaken hole only produces one thing— *trash.*" That's what Uncle Pete and Uncle Bert always said about the Hollow. And because everybody knew Roanie Sullivan was trash—came from it, looked like it, and smelled like it—they steered clear of him in the crowd. Maybe that was one reason I couldn't take my eyes off him. We were both human islands stuck in the middle of a lonely, embarrassing sea of space.

My cousin Carlton lounged a couple of feet away, between Roanie and the Jaycees' table. There are some relatives you just tolerate, and Carlton Maloney was in that group. He was about twelve, smug and well-fed, and he was laughing at me so hard that his eyes nearly disappeared in his face. He and my brother Hop were in the seventh grade together. Hop said he cheated on math tests. He was a weasel.

I saw him glance behind him. Once, twice. Uncle Dwayne was in charge of the Jaycees' food table and Aunt Rhonda was talking to him about something, so he was looking at her dutifully. He'd left a couple of dollar bills beside the cardboard shoe box he was using as a cash till.

Carlton eased one hand over, snatched the money, and stuck it in his trouser pocket.

I was stunned. He'd stolen from the Jaycees. He'd stolen from his own *uncle*. My brothers and I had been trained to such a strict code of honor that we wouldn't pilfer so much as a penny from the change cup on Daddy's dresser. I admit I had a weakness for the bags of chocolate chips in the bakery section of the grocery store, and if one just *happened* to fall off the shelf and burst open, I'd sample a few. But nonedible property was sacred. And stealing *money* was unthinkable.

Uncle Dwayne looked down at the table. He frowned. He hunted among packages of sugar cookies wrapped in cellophane and tied with green ribbons. He leaned toward Carlton and said something to him. From the stage I couldn't hear what he said—I couldn't hear anything except the music pounding in my ears—but I saw Carlton draw back dramatically, shaking his head. Then he turned and pointed at Roanie.

I was struck tapless. I simply couldn't move a foot. I stood there, rooted in place, and was dimly, painfully aware of people laughing at me, of my grandparents hiding their smiles behind their hands, and of Mama's and

Daddy's bewildered stares. Daddy, who could not dance either, waved his big hands helpfully, as if I was a scared calf he could shoo into moving again.

But I wasn't scared. I was furious.

Uncle Dwayne, his jaw thrust out, pushed his way around the table and grabbed Roanie by one arm. I saw Uncle Dwayne speak forcefully to him. I saw the blank expression on Roanie's face turn to sullen anger. I guess it wasn't the first time he'd been accused of something he didn't do.

His eyes darted to Carlton. He lunged at him. They went down in a heap, with Carlton on the bottom. People scattered, yelling. The whole Leprechaun Review came to a wobbly halt. Aunt Gloria bounded to her portable record player and the music ended with a screech like an amplified zipper. I bolted down the stairs at that end of the stage and squirmed through the crowd of adults.

Uncle Dwayne was trying to pull Roanie off Carlton, but Roanie had one hand wound in the collar of Carlton's sweater. He had the other at Carlton's throat, with the point of a rusty little penknife poised beneath Carlton's Adam's apple. "I didn't take no money!" Roanie yelled at him. "You damn liar!"

Daddy plowed into the action. He planted a knee in Roanie's back and wrenched the knife out of his hand. He and Uncle Dwayne pried the boys apart, and Daddy pulled Roanie to his feet. "He has a knife," I heard someone whisper. "That Sullivan boy's vicious."

"Where's that money?" Uncle Dwayne thundered, peering down into Roanie Sullivan's face. "Give it to me. Right now."

"I ain't got no money. I didn't take no money." He mouthed words like a hillbilly, kind of honking them out half finished. He had a crooked front tooth with jagged edges, too. It flashed like a lopsided fang.

"Oh, yeah, you did," Carlton yelled. "I saw you! Everybody knows you steal stuff! Just like your daddy!"

"Roanie, hand over the money," Daddy said. Daddy had a booming voice. He was fair, but he was tough. "Don't make me go through your pockets," he added sternly. "Come on, boy, tell the truth and give the money back."

"I ain't *got* it."

I was plastered to the sidelines but close enough to see the misery and defensiveness in Roanie's face. Oh, lord. He was the kind of boy who fought and cussed and put a knife to people's throats. He caused trouble. He deserved trouble.

But he's not a thief.

Don't tattle on Carlton. Maloneys stick together. We're big, that way.

But it's not fair.

"All right, Roanie," Daddy said, and reached for the back pocket of Roanie's dirty jeans.

"He didn't take it," I said loudly. "Carlton did!" Everyone stared at me. Well, I'd gotten used to that. I met Roanie Sullivan's wary, surprised eyes. He could burn a hole through me with those eyes.

Uncle Dwayne glared at me. "Now, Claire. Are you sure you're not getting back at Carlton because he spit boiled peanuts at you outside Sunday school last week?"

No, but I knew how a boiled peanut felt. Hot, real hot. "Roanie didn't take the money," I repeated. I jabbed a finger at Carlton. "Carlton did. I *saw* him, Daddy. I saw him stick it in his front pocket."

Daddy and Uncle Dwayne pivoted slowly. Carlton's face, already sweaty and red, turned crimson. "*Carlton,*" Uncle Dwayne said.

"She's just picking on me!"

Uncle Dwayne stuck a hand in Carlton's pocket and pulled out two wadded-up dollar bills.

And that was that.

Uncle Dwayne hauled Carlton off to find Uncle Eugene and Aunt Arnetta, Carlton's folks. Daddy let go of Roanie Sullivan. "Go on. Get out of here."

"He pulled that knife, Holt," Uncle Pete said behind me.

Daddy scowled. "He couldn't cut his way out of a paper sack with a knife that little."

"But he *pulled* it on Carlton."

"Forget about it, Pete. Go on, everybody."

Roanie stared at me. I held his gaze as if hypnotized. Isolation radiated from him like an invisible shield, but there was this *gleam* in his eyes, made up of surprise and gratitude and suspicion, bearing on me like concentrated fire, and I felt singed. Daddy put a hand on the collar of the faded, floppy football jersey he wore and dragged him away. I started to follow, but Mama had gotten through the crowd by then, and she snagged me by the back of my dress. "Hold on, Claire Karleen Maloney. You've put on enough of a show."

Dazed, I looked up at her. Hop and Evan peered at me from her side. Violet and Rebecca watched me, open-mouthed. A whole bunch of Maloneys scrutinized me. "Carlton's a weasel," I explained finally.

Mama nodded. "You told the truth. That's fine. You're done. I'm proud of you."

"Then how come everybody's lookin' at me like I'm weird?"

"Because you *are*," Rebecca blurted out. "Aren't you scared of Roanie Sullivan?"

"He didn't laugh at me when I was dancing. I think he's okay."

"You've got a strange way of sortin' things out," Evan said.

"She's one brick short of a load," Hop added.

So that was the year I realized Roanie was not just trashy, not just different, he was dangerous, and taking his side was a surefire way to seed my own mild reputation as a troublemaker and Independent Thinker.

I was fascinated by him from then on.

"An enthralling tale of two compelling, heartwarming characters and the healing power of love . . . I loved it!"—Elizabeth Thornton, author of *You Only Love Twice*

The historical tales of Karyn Monk are filled with unforgettable romance and her own special brand of warmth and humor. Now love casts its spell in the Highlands, as a warrior seeks a miracle from a mysterious lady of secrets and magic. . . .

The Witch and the Warrior
BY KARYN MONK

Suspected of witchcraft, Gwendolyn MacSween has been con-demned to being burned at the stake at the hands of her own clan. Yet rescue comes from a most unlikely source. Mad Alex MacDunn, laird of the mighty rival clan MacDunn, is a man whose past is scarred with tragedy and loss. His last hope lies in capturing the witch of the MacSweens—and using her magic to heal his dying son. He expects to find an old hag. . . . Instead he finds a young woman of unearthly beauty. There's only one problem: Gwendolyn has no power to bewitch or to heal. Now she must pretend to be a sorceress—or herself perish. But can she use her common sense to save Alex's son, and her natural powers as a woman to enchant a fierce and handsome Highland warrior—before a dangerous enemy destroys them both?

Gwendolyn regarded the sky in bewilderment. She had never witnessed such an abrupt change in the weather.

"Everything is fine," she assured them loudly. "The spirits have heard my plea."

They remained in their circle, watching the sky as a cool gale whipped their hair and clothes. And then, just as suddenly as it burst upon them, the storm died. The wind gasped and was gone, and the clouds melted into the darkness, unveiling the silent, tranquil glow of the moon and stars once again.

"By God, that was something!" roared Cameron, slapping Brodick heartily on the back. "Have you ever seen such a thing?"

"Did you see that, Alex?" demanded Brodick, looking uneasy.

"Aye," said Alex. "I saw."

Brodick raised his arm and cautiously flexed it at the elbow. "I think my arm feels better." He sounded more troubled than pleased.

"I *know* my head feels better!" said Cameron happily. "What about you, Neddie?"

"I have no wounds for the witch to heal," said Ned, shrugging. He frowned, then shrugged again. "That's odd," he remarked, slowly turning his head from side to side. "My neck has been stiff and aching for a week, and suddenly it feels fine."

Gwendolyn folded her arms across her chest and regarded them triumphantly. Clearly just the suggestion that they would feel better had had an effect on them, which was what she had hoped would happen. Luckily, the weather had complemented her little performance.

"Can you cast that spell on anyone?" asked Cameron, still excited.

"Not everyone," she replied carefully. "And my spells don't always work."

"What do you mean?" demanded Alex.

"The success of a spell depends on many things," she replied evasively. She did not want him to think she could simply say a few words and fell an entire army. "My powers will not work on everyone."

"I don't give a damn if they work on everyone," he growled. "As long as they work on one person." His expression was harsh. "Cameron, take the first watch. The rest of you get some sleep. We ride at first light."

Brodick produced an extra plaid from his horse and carefully draped it over Isabella's unconscious form. Then he lay down just a few feet away from her, where he could watch over her during the night. Ned and MacDunn also stretched out upon the ground, arranging part of their plaids over their shoulders for warmth.

"Do you sleep standing up?" MacDunn asked irritably.

"No," replied Gwendolyn.

"Then lie down," he orderd. "We still have a long journey ahead."

She had assumed they were going to bind her to a tree. But with Cameron watching her, she would not get very far if she attempted to escape tonight. Obviously that was what MacDunn believed. Relieved that she would not be tied, she wearily lowered herself to the ground.

Tomorrow would be soon enough to find an opportunity for escape.

The little camp grew quiet, except for the occasional snap of the fire. Soon the rumble of snoring began to drift lazily through the air. Gwendolyn wondered how they had all managed to find sleep so quickly in such uncomfortable conditions. The fire had died and the ground was damp and cold, forcing her to curl into a tight ball and wrap her bare arms around herself. It didn't help. With every passing moment her flesh grew more chilled, until finally her entire body was shivering uncontrollably.

"Gwendolyn," called MacDunn in a low voice, "come here."

She sat up and peered at him through the darkness. "Why?" she demanded suspiciously.

"Because your chattering teeth are keeping me awake," he grumbled. "You will lie next to me and share my plaid."

She stared at him in horror. "I am fine, MacDunn," she hastily assured him. "You needn't concern yourself about—"

"Come here," he repeated firmly.

"No," she replied, shaking her head. "I may be your prisoner, but I will *not* share your bed."

She waited for him to argue. Instead he muttered something under his breath, adjusted his plaid more to his liking over his naked chest and closed his eyes once again. Satisfied that she had won this small but critical battle, she vigorously rubbed her arms to warm them, then primly curled onto the ground.

Her teeth began to chatter so violently she had to bite down hard to try to control them.

The next thing she knew, MacDunn was stretching out beside her and wrapping his plaid over both of them.

"Don't you dare touch me!" Gwendolyn hissed, rolling away.

MacDunn grabbed her waist and firmly drew her back, imprisoning her in the warm crook of his enormous, barely clad body.

"Be still!" he ordered impatiently.

"I will not be still, you foul, mad ravisher of women!" She kicked him as hard as she could in his shin.

"Jesus—" he swore, loosening his hold slightly.

Gwendolyn tried to scramble away from him, but he instantly tightened his grip.

"Listen to me!" he commanded, somehow managing to keep his voice low. "I have no intention of bedding you, do you understand?"

Gwendolyn glared at him, her breasts rising and falling so rapidly they grazed his bandaged chest.

"I may be considered mad," he continued, "but to my knowledge I have not yet earned a reputation as a ravager of unwilling women—do you understand?"

His blue eyes held hers. She tried to detect deceit in them, but could not. All she saw was anger, mingled with weariness.

"I have already risked far more than I have a right to, to save your life and take you home with me, Gwendolyn MacSween," he continued. "I will *not* have it end by watching you fall deathly ill from the chill of the night."

He waited a moment, allowing his comments to penetrate her fear. Then, cautiously, he loosened his grip. "Lie still," he ordered gruffly. "I will keep you warm, nothing more. You have my word."

She regarded him warily. "You swear you will not abuse me, MacDunn? On your honor?"

"I swear."

Reluctantly, she eased herself onto her side. MacDunn adjusted part of his plaid over her, then once again fitted himself around her. His arm circled her waist, drawing her into the warm, hard cradle of his body. Gwendolyn lay there rigidly for a long while, scarcely breathing, waiting for him to break his word.

Instead, he began to snore.

Heat seemed to radiate from him, slowly permeating

her chilled flesh. It warmed even the soft wool of his plaid, she realized, snuggling further into it. A deliciously masculine scent wafted around her, the scent of horse and leather and woods. Little by little, the feel of MacDunn's powerful body against hers became more comforting than threatening, especially as his snores grew louder.

Until that moment, she had had virtually no knowledge of physical contact. Her mother had died when she was very young, and her father, though loving, had never been at ease with open demonstrations of affection. The unfamiliar sensation of MacDunn's warm body wrapped protectively around her was unlike anything she had ever imagined. She was his prisoner. And yet, she felt impossibly safe.

"You belong to me now," he had told her. *"I protect what is mine."* She belonged to no one. She reflected drowsily, and no one could protect her from men like Robert, or the ignorance and fear that was sure to fester in MacDunn's own clan the moment they saw her. She would escape him long before they reached his lands. Tomorrow, she would break free from these warriors, so she could retrieve the stone, return to her clan and kill Robert. Above all else, Robert must die. She would make him pay for murdering her father and destroying her life.

But all this seemed distant and shadowy as she drifted into slumber, sheltered by this brave, mad warrior, whose heart pulsed steadily against her back.

On sale in June:

GENUINE LIES
by *Nora Roberts*

THE HOSTAGE BRIDE
by *Jane Feather*

THE WEDDING CHASE
by *Rebecca Kelley*

Bestselling Historical Women's Fiction

✴ AMANDA QUICK ✴

____28354-5 SEDUCTION . . .$6.50/$8.99 Canada

____28932-2 SCANDAL . . . .$6.50/$8.99

____28594-7 SURRENDER . . . .$6.50/$8.99

____29325-7 RENDEZVOUS . . . .$6.50/$8.99

____29315-X RECKLESS . . . .$6.50/$8.99

____29316-8 RAVISHED . . . .$6.50/$8.99

____29317-6 DANGEROUS . . . .$6.50/$8.99

____56506-0 DECEPTION . . . .$6.50/$8.99

____56153-7 DESIRE . . . .$6.50/$8.99

____56940-6 MISTRESS . . . .$6.50/$8.99

____57159-1 MYSTIQUE . . . .$6.50/$7.99

____57190-7 MISCHIEF . . . .$6.50/$8.99

____57407-8 AFFAIR . . . .$6.99/$8.99

✴ IRIS JOHANSEN ✴

____29871-2 LAST BRIDGE HOME . . .$5.50/$7.50

____29604-3 THE GOLDEN

               BARBARIAN . . . .$6.99/$8.99

____29244-7 REAP THE WIND . . . . .$5.99/$7.50

____29032-0 STORM WINDS . . . .$6.99/$8.99

Ask for these books at your local bookstore or use this page to order.

Please send me the books I have checked above. I am enclosing $____ (add $2.50 to cover postage and handling). Send check or money order, no cash or C.O.D.'s, please.

Name _____

Address _____

City/State/Zip _____

Send order to: Bantam Books, Dept. FN 16, 2451 S. Wolf Rd., Des Plaines, IL 60018
Allow four to six weeks for delivery.

Prices and availability subject to change without notice.   FN 16 3/98

Bestselling Historical Women's Fiction

❧ IRIS JOHANSEN ❧

____28855-5 THE WIND DANCER . . .$5.99/$6.99

____29968-9 THE TIGER PRINCE . . .$6.99/$8.99

____29944-1 THE MAGNIFICENT

              ROGUE . . . .$6.99/$8.99

____29945-X BELOVED SCOUNDREL .$6.99/$8.99

____29946-8 MIDNIGHT WARRIOR . .$6.99/$8.99

____29947-6 DARK RIDER . . . .$6.99/$8.99

____56990-2 LION'S BRIDE . . . .$6.99/$8.99

____56991-0 THE UGLY DUCKLING. . .$5.99/$7.99

____57181-8 LONG AFTER MIDNIGHT.$6.99/$8.99

____10616-3 AND THEN YOU DIE.... $22.95/$29.95

❧ TERESA MEDEIROS ❧

____29407-5 HEATHER AND VELVET .$5.99/$7.50

____29409-1 ONCE AN ANGEL . . . . .$5.99/$7.99

____29408-3 A WHISPER OF ROSES .$5.99/$7.99

____56332-7 THIEF OF HEARTS . . . .$5.50/$6.99

____56333-5 FAIREST OF THEM ALL .$5.99/$7.50

____56334-3 BREATH OF MAGIC . . .$5.99/$7.99

____57623-2 SHADOWS AND LACE . .$5.99/$7.99

____57500-7 TOUCH OF

              ENCHANTMENT. . . . .$5.99/$7.99

Ask for these books at your local bookstore or use this page to order.

Please send me the books I have checked above. I am enclosing $____ (add $2.50 to cover postage and handling). Send check or money order, no cash or C.O.D.'s, please.

Name _____

Address _____

City/State/Zip _____

Send order to: Bantam Books, Dept. FN 16, 2451 S. Wolf Rd., Des Plaines, IL 60018

Allow four to six weeks for delivery.

Prices and availability subject to change without notice.   FN 16 3/98